Not Quite Good Enough

by *T' La June*

The Alter Ego of Toi Moore

TM Publications
Sun City, California, USA

Not Quite Good Enough
by *T' La June*

The Alter Ego of Toi Moore

All Rights Reserved. Copyright 2010, Toi Moore
ISBN 978-0-9713221-5-8
First Printing, June 2010
Copyright Toi Moore, 2010
Printed in the United States of America

Published by:
TM PUBLICATIONS
P.O. Box 2099
Sun City, CA 92586-2099
TMPublications1@aol.com

Visit our Web site at: http://www.ToiMoore.com

Front Cover Model:
Dorian Drake
Back Cover Model:
John Brice
Cover Layout:
Laurice Richie
Art Work
Leonard Ragsdale

Editors:
M.S. Bratton
Renee Keeble
Margarita Sweet
Charlene Tisdale

All rights reserved. No part of this book may be reproduced, stored in or introduced into a retrieval system, or transmitted, in any form, or by any means (electronic, mechanical, photocopying, recording, or otherwise), without written permission of both the copyright owner and the publisher, except in the case of quotes used in critical articles and reviews.

This book is a work of fiction. Names, characters, places and incidents either are products of the author's imagination or are used fictitiously. Any resemblance to actual events or locales or persons, living or dead, is entirely coincidental.

For MATURE AUDIENCES ONLY!

Due to the sexual content in this book, it is NOT

recommended that anyone with sexual

hang-ups read this material

as it may be offensive.

If this is YOU,

put the book down NOW and walk away!

****

If it is NOT YOU, what are you waiting for,

get to reading,

you're missing out on ALL the fun! LOL :)

Enjoy your read as much as

I enjoyed creating a funny and erotic story!

T' La June

Dedication

Gregory "G. Moe" Moore, I dedicate this book to YOU! Honey, you are my EVERYTHING! There would be no me, without YOU! I would like to THANK YOU first for being YOU! I knew we had something VERY special from the first day we met on September 11, 1982, when we shared our very first kiss. We have been kissing ever since.:) Since that day you have ALWAYS supported me and been by my side! No words will ever be able to express the gratitude and love I have for YOU!

Throughout our twenty-seven plus years of being together as a couple, you have ALWAYS encouraged me to FOLLOW MY DREAMS, DO WHAT I ENJOY, and NEVER ALLOW ANYONE TO BREAK MY SPIRIT WITH NEGATIVITY! I thank you for that honey!
I lean on you with everything I have, knowing that you are ALWAYS going to be there to lift me up, love me, and carry me through!
We are a team, soul-mates, best friends, and lovers!

Greg, I am VERY PROUD of YOU, WHAT YOU STAND FOR, BELIEVE IN, and how you've always PROVIDED FOR ME AND OUR SON'S!
I LOVE YOU ALWAYS! Thanks for those RESEARCH/STUDY nights we shared while I wrote this book. WE had FUNNN and continue to share in that fun as I research/study for my next book! Who said old married couples can't have fun? Not us! LOL
Here's to another twenty-plus years of love!

For you, my Prince Charming,
YOU ARE QUITE GOOD ENOUGH AND MOORE!
I Love you always Honey!
Toi

Chapters

Preface

1.) Super Large Penis — 1

2.) The Brush-off — 8

3.) Desperate and Horny — 13

4.) Listen Here Bitches — 17

5.) Taken or Gay? — 22

6.) Thick Rich Chocolate Stick — 30

7.) I Want Some Dick Too — 41

8.) Gigolo Hoe — 43

9.) Naked and Hot! — 45

10.) The Climax — 54

11.) One Night Stand — 61

12.) The Make-Over — 68

13.) The Hook Up — 80

14.) Mystery Caller — 83

Chapters

15.) Wanna Play House?   85

16.) Five Minute Sex   87

17.) Did He Make You Holler?   90

18.) Sexual Pleasures   92

19.) Why Bring Candy to a Candy Store?   93

20.) The Booty Call   98

21.) Sexual Delight   104

22.) The Three-Some   105

23.) He Can't Please Me   113

24.) Better Than a Dildo   116

25.) Bad-Ass Kids   120

26.) Sex Gadgets   122

27.) We're Pregnant   125

28.) The Big Party   133

29.) One Year Later   159

Preface

Get ready for a GREAT time when reading *Not Quite Good Enough*! I had sooooo much fun writing this book. With four published books under my belt, this is the first novel that I found myself repeatedly laughing out loud while writing! Several nights, after writing chapters of *Not Quite Good Enough* I went searching for my husband, Greg, who later fell asleep wearing a large smile! :)

My alter ego, *T'LaJune*, came FULLY ALIVE when writing this novel. This personality unleashed my EROTIC, and sometimes OVER the line personality. Besides, God didn't give us sensuous and sexual feelings to keep them hidden deep inside!:)

The comments I received from the few select friends and editors, who read my entire book or small portions before published, assured me that what I was writing was entertaining, amazing, unusual, and out of this world, for my usual writing style. One friend called and said, "What are you and Greg doing over there because you're writing porn!"
I simply told her,
"We're working on making our marriage last for **ANOTHER 25 PLUS YEARS!**"

One of my editors told me during her reading, "I was editing while I was at work and found myself laughing out loud!
I had to close my office door when
I remembered I was still at work!"

Another editor told me, "When I started reading I wasn't sure if I should blush or be embarrassed, because this isn't like any of your other books. Then I couldn't put the book down. After editing, I found myself laughing at some of the stories/characters as I went through my day!" While dealing with a family crisis, another editor said; "I'm sooo happy I'm editing this book. It has kept me laughing and has lifted up my spirits while dealing with pain and tragedy."

These thoughts reassured me that I was doing what I love to do, CREATE! It was making people smile while enjoying my journey. I just wanted to say thank you for the support you're giving me with your purchase of *Not Quite Good Enough* and the past purchases of my other books. To my die hard fans and/or past supporters, this novel is unlike ANY book I've ever written, so you'll be totally surprised! Another editor summed it all up by saying, "You're just like an actor, it's not YOUR life, you just got into CHARACTER and had fun while writing."

Who would have known I had a comedic style hidden inside? Who would have known I had such an erotic flavor deep within? Who would have known I could tie the two worlds of erotica and comedy relief together and make them work? I sure didn't know until I wrote *Not Quite Good Enough!* All I can say is I had a ballllll learning that I was able to fall DEEP into my characters and had funnnn making them come alive! I hope you enjoy reading this book as much as I had fun writing it!

Remember, this book is for
MATURE READERS ONLY!
So watch out, you're in for a ride of SEXUAL FANTASY and HUMOR!
In *Not Quite Good Enough*, you will enjoy a laugh, seek a partner/toy for romance, or experience pure down-right HOT AND HEAVY SEX!

Not Quite Good Enough
is where **EROTICA MEETS COMEDY WITH A BANGGGG!**

You are now entering into a world of **LAUGHTER and SEX!**

Not Quite Good Enough

by *T' La June*
The Alter Ego of Toi Moore

FOR MATURE READERS ONLY!

Thoughts from the Editors on *Not Quite Good Enough*

Renee Keeble
"While reading *Not Quite Good Enough,* I found myself eagerly awaiting the next chapter. I realized even more that gay doesn't always mean happy."

M.S. Bratton
"I didn't know whether to cover my eyes or blush with school girl embarrassment when I started reading *Not Quite Good Enough*. Then I couldn't stop turning each heat filed page."

Margarita Sweet
"*Not Quite Good Enough,* the ascent and descent of relationships and self-esteem told through the stories of characters who will make you laugh, frown & cry and when it's all over restore your belief in the power of love."

Charlene Tisdale
"*Not Quite Good Enough* is a story that will have you laughing hard and at the same time, wanting to jump inside the book to shake the character. I couldn't put the book down."

To My Editors:
I would like to personally thank each of you for helping me with this book. Your input helped to make my book extra special! You guys came through with flying colors!
I TRULY APPRECIATE your help, the time you put into your edits, your suggestions, and feedback. I also enjoyed reading and/or listening to your thoughts and how you enjoyed **NOT QUITE GOOD ENOUGH** while editing! Now, I'm ready to share my fun and romance with the WORLD!
Thanks again!
Toi aka T' LaJune :)

Not Quite Good Enough

One - *Super Large Penis*

"Girlll come over here and look at this shit. Damnnn!!" Marque' said to Mae May, as he blushes with amazement while caressing a lustful sex gadget at the *Lotion in Motion Erotic Store* in Hollywood, California. "Yummy, yummy, yummy!" He continues as they laugh, making sexual gestures while looking at a super large penis that has a real and natural texture, just like you were caressing a man's most private and intimate desires.

"Girlllll, I can work wonders with this long brown thang," Marque' swears as he turns the speed control on to HIGH where it produces an erotic, delightfully vibrating, and out of this world sensation! The high speed controller generates a pleasure toy that motions an up and down throbbing feeling which creates an in and out fantasy of making love. "Ah shit, this thang feels good!" He moans while rolling his eyes around his head, indicating pure pleasure. "This thang feels soooo real I could eat it for dinner!" Marque' admits as he gently caresses the tester from top to bottom, enjoying its natural, powerful feel, and motions.

The tall, dark, and handsome 33 year old well groomed, attractive, flamboyant gay man, opens a tube of an oily cream, squeezing it into his hands. Marque' slowly massages it onto the penis, stroking it up and down, until the entire shaft heats up and tingles with excitement, making the experience even more erotic and intimate. "Damnnnnnn, this feels good, damnnnnn!" he pleasantly confesses. Next, he sticks out his tongue like he's licking the tip of the penis in a circular motion while displaying facial expressions of sexual gratification with his eyes. Then he opens his mouth wide and motions an erotic illusion of a well endowed penis traveling down his throat as if it were embracing every inch buried deep inside.

T' La June

Marque's 31 year old, loud talking, ghetto fabulous best friend, Mae May, is used to the great sense of humor he often flaunts and laughs, "Damnnnn Marque', you're crazy as hell!" Mae May said while trying to snatch the gadget out of his hand. "Give it here. I need to try out this dildo myself tonight!"

Marque' quickly pulls away, "Hell no you can't have it, I need this thang my own damn self. Bitch, get your own." he teases. Then with an embarrassing expression, he watches the tester fall to the floor as it slides out his hand, "Oh shit, I'm getting ready to damage perfection," he jokes. He quickly picks up the penis, places it back on the shelf, grabs an unopened package, and gives it to Mae May. "Just kidding girl, here you go. I already have one at home and believe me, it has powers like you'd never believe."

Mae May is not surprised by Marque's admission and asks, "Just how much power does it have?" She runs her three inch long, multi-colored, diamond-studded, fingernails up and down the powerful long brown shaft for inspection. "Damn, I really do like this thang!" She pleasantly responds as she considers the item even more.

As Marque' watches the excited look on Mae May's face, he adds, "This sucker has more power than anything you've ever used. And please believe what I'm telling you." Marque' swears as he puts one hand on his hip and the other against his face as he remembers, "Ummm, come to think of it, the one I have IS rather old and quite run down." He displays a devilish grin and continues, "So I DO need to get another one. Shittt, I've worn the hell out of that thang!" The two beauty shop workers laugh out loud as they each put a penis in their baskets and continue looking at other gadgets in the store.

"Marque' look at this. Do you have one of these?" Mae May said with excitement as she holds up a super large battery operated

Not Quite Good Enough

rabbit. The rabbit has four levels of power ranging from low to extra high with a buzzing affect that could stimulate a mating call for a swarm of killer bees.

Marque' picks up the sex toy and flashes a large grin.

"No, I don't have this one. But it looks like it will be an extra special something, something for me and my man tonight. Shitttt, we're gonna have a good ole' time with this thang." Marque' puts the gadget in his basket as they continue looking through the store.

As the two laugh and make sexual gestures with the many erotic toys, Mae May notices two women whispering and looking at them frowning. Mae May puts her hand on her hip, throws her head back, rolls her eyes, and talks out loud. "Excuse me, I said excuse me!" She said with an angry tone while giving the ladies an evil look. The ladies quickly turn the other way, trying to act like they didn't hear her.

"What's the matter?" Marque' asks.

"Those two bitches over there are trippin' and I'm not having it, hell to the nawww!" Mae May says, then blurts out louder, "I said excuse me you two BITCHES in the tacky looking shorts and tank tops! I know you hear me because you were all in my kool-aid a few minutes ago when I wasn't talking to you. So why you trying to act like you don't hear me now?"

Other people in the store are now looking so Mae May looks around and aims her conversation at everyone, "What ya'll looking at? I'm not talking to any of you so turn back around and get out my business. I'm talking to the tacky lookin' white bitches with the dull and trashy looking weaves in their hair and the fucked up nails."

Afraid of what may happen, everyone turns away from Mae May's view as she continues. "Hey you white pieces of trash, you didn't seem to have a problem hearing me awhile ago when I was minding my own damn business. Now you're acting like you don't hear me and I'm talking loud enough so you can. Say something now, or better yet, look over here again and turn your noses down at us and you'll see what's gonna happen to you. Come on bitches, try me." Mae May puts her hands high in the air, displaying gang signs, and gestures ready for a fight.

"Yeah, you heard her. Say something or look over here again so we can come over there and start kicking some ass!" Marque' adds.

Suddenly the ladies notice Marque' and Mae May coming toward them. They drop what's in their hands and run out the store. Marque' and Mae May follow them to the door and Mae May yells, "Yeah, and don't let me see you again or I'll kick your ass!" The ladies jump into a red sports car and speed out the parking lot. Mae May looks at Marque' and they laugh as they give each other a high five and go back to shopping. The rest of the store customers again turn away from Mae May and Marque's direction, keeping a safe distance from the pair.

Once they're finished shopping they bring their items to the counter to pay. "Damn ya'll," the store manager greets them with a serious tone. "Every time you guys come in here there's some shit."

"Fuck you Jimmy," Marque' jokes as he and Mae May give their favorite store manager a hug.

"I know you guys are some of our best customers, but damn, don't run away all of our new customers." Jimmy jokes.

"Like I said earlier, fuck you Jimmy! Just ring up my shit so I can get out of your ghetto ass store," Marque' again jokes as Mae May and Jimmy laugh while he rings up their items.

"If our store is so ghetto then how come ya'll always got ya'll's crazy asses up in here?" Jimmy sarcastically fires back and laughs.

Marque' begins flirting with the medium built, brown-skin,

Not Quite Good Enough

handsome 30 year old man. "Because I'm waiting for you to come over my house and help me break-in the toys I've been buying." Marque' jokes.

Jimmy responds, "Marque', I told you I have a man that I'm faithful to, so you will have to wait and see what happens between me and my man. Besides, I'm not a hoe like you," he teases. "I'm a one man's man. When I'm committed to someone, I'm committed."

"Okkkk Jimmy boy, I heard that line before." Marque' rolls his eyes and smirks as he continues. "All I have to say is you don't know what you're missing, missy!" Marque' blinks and blows Jimmy a kiss as he puts the last item in the bag.

Mae May rolls her eyes, shakes her head, and jokes, "Damn ya'll, I don't want to hear all this shit again. Jimmy, just hurry up and break up with your man so you can make Marque' happy."

Jimmy takes his hands, caresses them along his body, holds his head up high and smiles, "They say good things are worth waiting for, so Marque' if you want me that bad, you'll just have to wait, because I know I'm a good catch!" He teases as Mae May and Marque' shake their heads and smile.

"Well then, I guess I'll never know if you don't break up with your man, or will I?" Marque' said as he reaches over the counter, grabs Jimmy's tie, pulls him close to his face, and kisses his lips, sticking his entire tongue in Jimmy's mouth, leaving both of them smiling.

Mae May grabs Marque's hand and pulls him away, "Come on Marque', let's go." Mae May said as she heads toward the door with Marque' following. "You guys are crazy." she jokes.

"It takes one to know one," Marque' responds to Mae May while still looking at Jimmy winking and blowing kisses. Once at the door, Marque' smiles at Jimmy, with Jimmy joining the gesture.

With an alluring tone, Marque' speaks loud enough for Jimmy

to hear him and says, "Come on Mae May, I can't wait to get home to try out my new gadgets, even if I have to try them out alone." Jimmy shakes his head and grins as Marque' adds, "See you next time sweetness and remember, I'll be waiting." Before walking out the door, Marque' winks again and blows Jimmy a kiss as they both blush.

When Marque' and Mae May are together, the sky is the limit as to the fun or madness they'll share. Marque' does hair and makeup at the *Sista Girls Salon and Barber Shop*, where he is the owner. The suave dresser only wears tightly fitted name brand clothes which draws attention with each stride of his walk. His seductive brown eyes draw attention to anyone within his glance, even causing women to take an extra glimpse before realizing he's gay and proud of it. His golden colored spiked hair is always perfectly groomed. He keeps his thick eyebrows arched, eyelashes thick with mascara, and his feet and nails perfectly manicured. He has double holes in each earlobe with platinum and diamond studded earrings. Marque's captivating and uplifting personality is out of this world, radiating confidence at it's best. Anyone in his presence is sure to be rejuvenated by the time they leave.

Marque's up-to-date and unique hair fashions keep him in high demand by the women. While his humor and lessons in finding and keeping a good man is his speciality. Most of the women who come into the salon have a hard time finding a good man, or keeping one in their bed. However, with Marque' being an expert in this field, makes it easy for him to give great advice and intimate details on what the ladies need to do to keep their men happy.

His surprising stories on what he does to please his boyfriends keep all ears wide open for full details, keeping the women puzzled with humor while he instructs them to do as he says AND as he does, in order for them to get a good man. Spotting a gay man from across the room is Marque's gift, allowing him to never be alone. Given his bold personality and highly confident attitude, when he sees someone he likes, he has no problem going after him.

When clients visit the *Sista Girls Salon and Barber Shop*, the women constantly find themselves seeking Marque's advice as they search for **Mr. Right** to show up in their lives instead of **Mr. Right Now**, whom they seem to meet on a continuous basis. As for Marque', with the many selections of men friends he entertains, he enjoys every lustful moment he shares with them, both privately and publically, while enjoying the savoring moments in the fine art of making love and pure downright sexual gratification.

Mae May is her name, but having wild sex tends to be her game! Mae May is the manicurist at the *Sista Girls Salon and Barber Shop*. Her bold and unusual nail designs keep both women and men coming back for fun. While her daring, outrageous, and ghetto fabulous style and personality keeps them laughing. Her unique manner also makes it hard for her to keep a man, or for them to take her serious.

She also has a hard time keeping a man because of her four bad-ass kids, who all have different daddy's. Her best friend, Marque', is the God-Father to her children. Mae May and her kids live with her mean-ass alcoholic momma, who takes care of the kids while she works. Mae May sports a multi-colored hair weave that proudly displays between three and four shades. Her loud and colorful makeup selection always matches her outrageous wardrobe selection. Her mascara is so thick that when she bats her eyes, they sling back in slow motion. Her bright red lipstick is sooo shiny that she looks like she's been eating fried chicken around the clock. Her unfashionably tacky flavored clothes cause many to take a second look. Her distinctive style and personality are something that only a confident woman would entertain the notion, making her an unusual sight to be seen.

T' La June

Her ghetto fabulous personality either makes you love her, or hate her. The voluptuous and over confident woman spends most of her money on her creatively fashioned wardrobe and partying, because the county welfare system supplies the needs of her children. She never leaves home without her makeup and hair fully intact. Her multi-hole giant hoop platinum earrings are a part of her signature look. Her distinguished nose and tongue rings always draw attention, causing her to boldly believe she's all that AND a bag of chips. She displays a large tattoo that's embedded across her lower back, just above her panty line, that exposes a colorful picture of her four children.

Another tattoo, shaped as a star, is positioned around her navel, decorated with a dangling diamond stud in the center. Each day before Mae May leaves the house she boldly models her curvaceous body in front of her full length mirror, puckers her lips as if she were ready for a juicy kiss, and winks her eye as a sign of approval, believing she's achieved total perfection, and then starts her day.

Clients know they are in for fun, excitement, and plenty of laughter when visiting the *Sista Girls Salon and Barber Shop*. Together, Marque' and Mae May are fun-filled, party going, free-spirited personalities who love to have a good time.

Not Quite Good Enough

Two - *The Brush-Off*

"Is there anything I can get you ladies?" The busboy says, flirting with Tammy who barely looks at the blushing, hardworking man. Tammy, a stuck-up and prissy acting gynecologist, is uninterested in having a conversation, responds with arrogance, "No thank you," and continues looking at her menu. Her best friend and co-worker Cindy, who's a receptionist in her doctor's office, smiles because of the unresponsive and rude looks Tammy is giving while hiding her head behind the menu.

Upset by her response, the busboy sits down two glasses of water so hard they make a loud bumping sound on the table and spill out. He responds, "Your waiter will be with you shortly," quickly walking away disappointed.

"Thank you." Tammy rudely says while Cindy quietly giggles.

"Girl, he was starring you down! He wants your body and he wants it bad!" Cindy teases.

"They all want my body." Tammy sarcastically jokes, then becomes arrogant, "Now tell me something I don't already know." She sips her water.

"Girlllll, I'm scared of you." Cindy teases

"Besides, it's something I get all the time."

"That's a shame." Cindy says while shaking her head grinning.

"What's a shame?" Tammy asks with a astonished look.

Cindy expresses her theory. "Tammy, you're always complaining about how you can't ever find a good man and when someone catches your eye you turn him down."

In a serious tone, Tammy defends herself. "Hell yeah I'm gonna turn down a damn busboy. I'm a 36 year old rich doctor who's worked hard to make my own money. Everything I have I've worked too hard to just give it away to some low-life that can spot a lady with money a mile away and then try to get a free ride on her dime. Hell, I ain't got time to give to the welfare system. Paying high taxes is enough," Tammy fumes and continues, "Next thing you know he'll be unemployed and looking at me to take care of his poor ass. Hell no!" The two laugh and continue looking at their menus while sitting at the table of a five star restaurant.

Tammy owns her own doctor's office in the high class neighborhood of Beverly Hills, California. She's very particular about the men she spends time with. She doesn't have a hard time attracting men because she's pretty, light-skinned, has long curly hair, thin, classy, and rich. She wears her make-up attractively appealing. Her hair and nails are always perfectly manicured. She fits perfectly in the itty-bitty-titty-committee with her A cup bra size. Her behind has a small curve, eliminating her from the well-endowed sista girl heritage. This combination makes the small curves on her body portionately appealing. However, with her conservative style of dressing that's always topped with fashionably styled high heels, lets those in her presence know that she settles for nothing less than the best.

However, most men can't please her because they don't make more money than she. When it comes to her money, she refuses to take care of a man, or his daily needs. The only men who can please her are those who are in her financial ball park or more, and will take anything she dishes out, which are generally white men. She feels the only thing a black man can offer her is good sex, so she uses them when she needs too. She's a very independent snob who doesn't have many friends. Her longtime family skeleton keeps her far away from her past.

Cindy is a 32 year old, average looking, prima-donna receptionist who doesn't make a lot of money. She lives from paycheck to paycheck, but shops like she's rich in order to keep up with Tammy's impressive lifestyle. She has a hard time getting

Not Quite Good Enough

a man because once they get to know her, they realize that all she wants is their money. She does everything she can to make Tammy proud of her. She even lies when needed to stay in Tammy's good grace.

As the two talk and laugh, the waiter comes to their table and takes their order. "Are you ladies ready to order?" he asks with a very proper tone.

"Yes," Tammy acknowledges as she gives him an order of steak, lobster, steamed vegetables, a baked potato, and red wine. Cindy follows her order, "I'll have what she's having." The waiter takes their menus and leaves the table.

Once he leaves, Cindy notices a well dressed brown-skinned, nicely-built, attractive man sitting across the room. He caught her attention because he kept smiling and staring at them. Cindy smiles and tells Tammy, "Look at that good looking man staring at me. He looks good enough to be my appetizer and dessert." she giggles.

Tammy looks to see what Cindy sees and notices the beaming bright smile of the handsome stranger. "Ummm, maybe!" Tammy reacts with an uninterested look while Cindy secretly flirts. Their food arrives and they begin to eat. While dining alone, the businessman passionately looks at them and continues to flirt.

Cindy continues to catch his eye looking at her while she eats, "Umm, umm, ummm! I may have to get his number when I leave." With a pessimistic tone, Tammy responds, "You go right ahead."

Once they finished eating, they pay their tab and begin to leave. The well dressed man suddenly gets up and follows them outside to the parking lot. "Excuse me ladies, I couldn't help but notice your beauty," he politely flirts.

Amused by his bold approach, Cindy flirts back, "We noticed you too."

Tammy casually acts like she notices the attention while

walking toward her car. "Hmm."

With a wide smile on his face, he quickly pulls out his business card and hands one to each of them. He begins to introduce himself, "My name is Joe Randall. Are you ladies single?"

Cindy quickly takes the card before Tammy and notice she's a sales assistant for a local unknown company. Suddenly she becomes uninterested and angry and gives back the card, "No we're not. Let's go Tammy."

Surprised by her reaction, Tammy quickly looks at her card, "She's right, we're not interested. In fact, you couldn't pay us enough money to be interested in you. You wouldn't be able to afford us anyway." Tammy throws down the card, and looks at Cindy as they walk away laughing, making him feel less than a proud man.

He picks up his card and becomes angry, defending himself by speaking out loud. "Oh, so it's like that? You don't have time for a hard working brotha like me?"

Tammy turns to look at Joe and says, "No, it's not like that at all." Joe smiles with hope from her response as she continues. "What it is, is that we don't have time for a Brotha who's somebody's damn assistant. Brotha you couldn't afford sistas like us if you tried. So don't waste our time or yours." They reach Tammy's bright red Mercedes. She unlocks the doors with her hand held remote control and they get inside.

Joe's ego is crushed, but he continues to defend himself before they drive off, "No, you get it straight Miss Stuck-Up-In-The-Ass Sista. You see, sistas like you are the reason brothas like me go white. You think you're too damn good for a working class man like me. You complain about not being able to get a good man, and I'm a damn good man! In fact, I'm more than good! Any sista with good sense would be proud to have me on her arm. But like I said earlier, that's why brothas like me go white, they treat us right!"

Not Quite Good Enough

"You can go white all you want because going white for me means I'll get taken care of hand and foot by the same man your white piece of trash didn't wait for. So, until you can take care of a sista hand and foot, keep a steppin' brotha," Tammy confidently says as her and Cindy continue to laugh, get into her car, slam the doors, and drive away leaving Joe standing alone and upset.

Joe shakes his head in disappointment and yells as they drive away, "That's alright, you sistas will be ole maids before you ever get someone as good as me to give you the time of day." He watches them fade into the sunset as he slowly walks to his car.

T' La June

Three - *Desperate and Horny*

"We should be getting some action real soon. If nothing else some free drinks. Just act cool," Sophia said to her best friend Vicki. They sit at the counter of a local bar, having a drink, waiting for a man to pick them up.

"Sophia, if I act any cooler I'll freeze." Vicki jokes as she looks around the room and notices that no one is paying them any attention. "Girl, we ain't going to catch a man by sitting at the bar like this. All they'll think is we're desperate and horny."

Sophia looks at her with a serious expression and jokes. "Well, we are."

"That doesn't mean we have to advertise that we are." Vicki, the 35 year old unlikeable busy body responds before getting up, "Let's go. Ain't nothing in this dark, old-ass, run down joint but some broke ass men who ain't got a pot to piss in. It makes no sense in wasting my time sitting here waiting for someone to pick me up. Hell, I don't know about you but I have a fully charged dildo waiting for me by my bed, so I'm outta here."

"You can leave if you want. But tonight I want me a real dick. So I'm staying until I find a man, goodbye." Sophia said as she takes the last drink of her whiskey and requests more. Vicki gets up feeling disappointed and leaves Sophia sitting at the bar drinking alone.

"Well, that's on you, I'll talk to you later." Vicki said as Sophia orders another drink. Vicki walks away and looks back at Sophia and thinks, "I may not be able to give you a real dick, but I can surely satisfy your sexual needs."

Adding to her unfriendly personality, Vicki's masculine looking characteristics make it very hard for her to attract a man. She wears little makeup and her hair in simple but groomed ponytail. Keeping up with fashions is not her cup-of-tea. The hardworking social

Not Quite Good Enough

worker makes a decent living. The well educated busybody thinks she has the right to analyze everyone by always criticizing and controlling their behavior. Vicki's always in someone's business, but refuses to tell any of hers. People wonder if she's gay or not because of her possessive and masculine ways. With Sophia being her best friend, many wonder if they are a couple on the down-low.

Sophia is a 37 year old confident lady who's round figure can easily fit into a size 2X. She's a plain looking lady who wears no make-up or jewelry. Her bushy eyebrows look like they haven't been maintained since birth. You will rarely find her in the chair of a beauty shop as she has no patience to groom herself to perfection. Her 46 triple D breast turn the heads of many when she wears low-cut, tight fitting clothes, however, she won't be caught wearing anything of the sorts.

Sophia has a problem with food by eating everything in sight when she's lonely and upset. Food has become her best friend. Even though she's very friendly and well liked, most men think of her as just one of the boy's and a close friend. Due to her weight issues and personal battles of insecurity, she's not a lady they'd romance or marry. In the past, Sophia has been known to romance women, even though she doesn't call herself a lesbian. The blue collar worker wears a man's uniform, a short masculine hairstyle, her perfume reeks the smell of recycled cans and bottles, and she wouldn't be caught dead wearing makeup. However, she is happy with herself and spends most of her free time with her friend Vicki.

Sophia questions herself as she continues sitting alone, drinking away her problems, "Damn, I've been sitting here for over an hour and no body's talking to me. I can't even get anyone to buy me a drink, damn! Maybe I should just go home and come back another night. At least Vicki was smart enough to leave before making herself look too desperate! When am I gonna get me a man, or better yet,

T' La June

when am I gonna get me some dick?" She slams down her glass, looks around the room to see if anyone notices her, and hopes for the best. "I guess if I were a wearing a size two, with long curly hair, and made a lot of money, I'd have as many men as I could handle. Let's face it, nobody wants a fat ass woman who lets the world know she can't find a good man."

While Sophia continues to wait, she grabs another handful of salty pretzels and stuffs them into her mouth. The longer she waits, the more she eats, attempting to melt her lonely and unwanted pains away.

Shortly after she gets an offer. "Hey lady, I see you're alone, would you like some company?" a drunken stranger suggests after stumbling to the bar for another round of drinks.

Vicki's not sure if she should be happy or sad with the approach. "Ahhh, sure." she hesitates.

The stranger sits down next to her and orders another round of drinks for both of them. "I want another whiskey and coke, and give the lady whatever she's having." He slurs as he quickly gulps down the last of his drink, waiting for the next round.

"Thank you." Vicki says, still feeling unsure about his company.

"You're welcomeeeee." He slurs, leans in close, and breathes his alcoholic breathe into her face. "So pretty lady, what's your name?" he asks as he hiccups the smell of whiskey.

While trying to avoid the awful smell, Vicki turns her head away and hesitantly answers, "Vicki and yours?" She frowns as she pulls back from him and the awful smell.

He leans back in, getting even closer than before, and breathes deeper into her face, "Tom, but my female friends call me Big Tom, if you know what I mean." he laughs with a hefty and sloppy tone.

"Ok, nice to meet you, I think." Vicki again leans away from him and takes a sip of her old drink when the new order arrives.

Not Quite Good Enough

"Thank you for the drink."

"You're welcome, cheers." He holds up his glass to hers. "Once we're done you can give me a little something, something to show your thanks." He winks at her.

Surprised by his comment, she questions his intentions. "Give you what?"

"I said you can give me a little something, something. Now listen here pretty lady, my female friends don't call me Big Tom for nothing if you know what I mean, and this drink ain't free. So, once you're done you're gonna pay for my hospitality." he smiles and loudly burps directly in her face, making her gag and almost throw up.

Vicki slams her drink down on the table and yells, "If you expect for me to pay you in sex then you can take your drink back." Suddenly she picks up the glass and throws her drink in his face.

Tom jumps up from the table in a rage, wipes his face with a napkin, and yells as Vicki is walking away, "You bitch! What you'd do that for? Ain't that the reason you're sitting here alone anyway? You want a man to rock your world, ain't that right?"

Vicki stops, looks at him, and with an angered attitude defends herself and says, "Are you calling me a hoe? Because if you were any kind of gentleman you would at least sweet talk me into WANTING to have sex with you. Instead, you buy me a six dollar drink and expect that I'm gonna have sex with your drunk ass. Hell, I'm at least worth dinner before giving it up."

The entire bar gets quiet as they listen to the conversation. Tom responds, "Lady, ain't nothing free anymore, so hell yeah I expect you to have sex with me after a six dollar drink. And if you want to be a hoe, that's fine with me too, just as long as you pay me back for my hospitality."

Vicki pulls out ten dollars from her purse and throws it at him, "Here's your lousy six dollars for the drink and a four dollar tip to get lost, you loser!" She heads toward the door feeling alone, disrespected, and disappointed.

Tom jokes before she leaves the room, "Hey, where you going? You didn't give me your address. I like a feisty woman with a lot of meat on her bones." he teases and continues. "We can have some real fun together. Come back." he yells as she storms toward the door.

Without looking back, Vicki gestures her middle figure toward him, "Fuck you." she yells back and keeps walking. Once at her car she feels bad. "The nerve of him. I should have known he was a loser when he came up to me smelling like a bottle of whiskey. Damn, I ain't that desperate. Oh well, so much for trying to find a man or even getting a man to make me feel good. I guess I'll just count tonight as another night of drinking, meeting losers, and eating my troubles away, damn, damn, damn!" She whines. "Oh well I tried. I needed to leave anyway so I can get my butt up for work in the morning, but first I wanna get something to eat. I think I'll get a few extra large pizzas, wings, some cherry cheesecake, and a couple gallons of butter pecan ice cream to wash away my pain. Since I didn't find a good man at least the food will make me feel good inside before I go to sleep." She starts up her car and heads toward the fast food store.

Not Quite Good Enough

Four - *Listen Here Bitches*

Several clients are in the *Sista Girls Salon and Barber Shop* getting their hair and nails groomed. The classy and upscale shop is filled with several pictures of distinguished African-Americans with chic hairstyles and haircuts. There is also a picture of President Barack Obama and First Lady, Michelle Obama on the wall as he takes his oath into office as the 44th president of United States of America; and the first African American president in the United States' history.

Marque' and Mae May are working on clients. As Marque' works on his client's hair he strikes up a new conversation with Mae May's client. "Girl, what's going on with you and your man this week? Did you ever convince him to go south on you?"

"Hell no! He just ain't having it. Said he wasn't brought up to do nasty things like that." Linda tells everyone as they laugh.

"Well I suggest you trade his ass in for a new joy stick because believe me, someone else will go South on you and enjoy every lick and taste, Ole'." Marque' raises his right hand in the air as to gesture a Mexican salute while everyone laughs and agrees.

"Amen!" Mae May throws up her hands. "If a brotha can't go South, then put his ass out, heyyyyy!" They laugh.

"Girl, you got to get a brotha that's going to please you, not tease you." Marque' insists.

"I hear what you're saying, but there ain't many good brothas out there these days. So I gotta take what I can get." Linda said, "Besides, most of them are locked up, or in your bed!" She laughs as she looks directly at Marque' sarcastically frowning.

"What can I say, the brothas come here to play and stay all damn day! Heyyy!!!" Marque' snaps his fingers in the air as they laugh.

"See, that's the problem, you got all the men. You never leave any for us," Linda adds. "Hell, I'm starting to think that there's no more straight brothas around because you've either changed their minds, or encouraged them to lose their minds."

"Linda, Linda, Lindaaa, girl, don't hate, just appreciate! Marque' teases.

"Appreciate what? Appreciate that you have all the men and us straight sistas can't find one good one?" Linda fires back.

"Appreciate that the ones I do have, you wouldn't want anyway. Orrrr, that the ones I have won't break your heart because they're too busy trying to get mine. Besides, that way you don't have to worry about one of them coming out the closet on you after you've fallen deeply in love, or break your heart. At least this way when you do find a man, ya'll know that he's straight and wants to be with you and only you."

"If you say so Missy," Linda says joking.

"Girl, ignore Marque', he talks just to hear his damn mouth running." Mae May adds with great sarcasm.

"Oh, oh, ohhhh, don't go there Miss Thang, please don't go there!" Marque' puts one hand on his side, tilts his back, raises the other hand that has his comb in it, high in the air and continues. "Especially after hearing about where your mouth was last night, the night before, and the night before that. So pleaseeeee don't go there Missy, or I'll be forced to tell all your damn secrets." Marque' clowns Mae May with a straight face. Everyone in the shop laughs and then looks at Mae May for details.

With a serious attitude Mae May fires back, "What ya'll looking at, I ain't got a damn thang to tell ya. So just turn ya'll's asses around and mind your own damn business." She smiles and continues doing her client's nails.

"Yeah, I thought you'd see things my way Missy!" Marque' teases and continues styling his clients hair.

Not Quite Good Enough

Mae May looks at Marque' and stands straight up from her chair, gestures her middle finger to say 'fuck you,' points it at him and continues, "Excuse me, I said excuseeeeee meeeee Marque'." Marque' and everyone in the shop stop what they're doing and look toward Mae May.

"Are you talking to me?" He asks with a confident attitude.

"If your name is Marque' then hell yeah I'm talking to you. Now don't forget about all the secrets I can tell about you Mister Missy, and you've got some good stories," she jokes.

"Excuse you sister, but I have nothing to hide because I've shared my entire life with everyone already. In fact, I'm the one who tells all you hussies what you need to do to get and keep a good man by my example. If it weren't for me all ya'll's asses wouldn't have a damn thang to talk about or look forward to hearing. Shittt, I'm the only one who keeps it's really real! I keep all the good shit going when it comes to hearing good gossip. Mae May you don't have anything to tell that would embarrass me because I put my own shit out there my damn self. But you on the other hand sista, I'd watch it, because YOU'VE got secrets that no one knows about BUT ME! Now, eat THAT apple pie and stuff it with some pride." Everyone laughs.

"All ya'll women ever do is complain about not being able to get a good man, or that someone ain't good enough for you." Everyone gets quiet with all eyes and ears focusing on Marque' as he explains his reality version of the birds and bees. "Listen here bitches, I'm gonna tell you something that will definitely blow your minds, so listen carefully because if you pay close attention you just might be able to get a good man. Now, I'm only gonna say this once, so pay close attention to what I'm saying and remember, DO as I say, AND as I DO!"

The entire shop gets quiet while focusing directly on Marque', "Now if ya'll women was going south on your man the right way, and

T' La June

I mean going wayyyy downnn to the deep south, and not just stopping at the boarder for a drop off, sucking his feet and toes like you were sipping an ice cream milkshake from a skinny straw, letting your tongue softly massage his legs up, down, inside and out like you were enjoying a hard red candy stick, you'd have a man. Then if you were working your tongue up to his nipples while rolling them in circles like you were trying to get down to the chocolate point in the center of his sugar-coated lollipop, then working your way up to his lips where your tongue would explode together with his like fireworks on the fourth of July, as your juices passionately savor the taste buds buried deep within the seas of your mouth, you'd have a man. Then when you're all done, roll over and let him smack that ass, you'd have a man. After you've warmed his pleasures up with joy, then let the same games occur on you, you'd have a man! Hell, they don't say, flip it, dip it, and rub it down for nothing!" After his explanation, the ladies' bodies begin sweating with excitement causing them to become out of breath, displaying constant panting motions which cause them to fan themselves, repeatedly, while waiting for it to be safe to come up for air. "Damnnnn!" Linda fans herself with a magazine.

"Wait, I'm not done." Marque' continues, "After you've turned each other on to extreme heights with the foreplay, the sex will be more than great, in fact it'll be out of this world. Fantastic!"

While everyone sits frozen in time, glued to Marque's every word, you could have heard a pin drop on the floor. "Once you've made love to each other like it's nobody's business and he rolls over to fall asleep with a big smile on his face, you'll have that man running back for more. Then get your ass up out of bed and make him a good home cooked meal. Feed him with your fingers, allowing him to lick every drip and crumb of food left behind. After all is said and done you'll always have a man in your bed, just like I do. In fact, you'll

Not Quite Good Enough

have him running back for more and more for the rest of your life! Shitttt, you'll have to have the cops put a restraining order on his ass if you ever want him to stay away." Marque' smiles and winks his eye to approve his statement as being a true fact.

Everyone is in shock and paralyzed to the vision Marque' displays as he continues. "Now you bitches see why I have all the men in my bed, why they stay so long, and why they always come back for more." He waves his hand high in the air, curving it side to side, and turns around to finish his client's hair.

"Damnnnnnnnn, I guess he told us, didn't he?" Linda says.

Mae May shakes her head, holds her head down, shuts her mouth, and quietly goes back to work.

"Hell, I may not have a man but after that explanation if I can't find one by tonight, I'm gonna have to use several battery operated toys just to satisfy my pleasure!" Linda teases while still fanning herself.

Marque' is smiling with pride while everyone laughs, shakes their heads in agreement, continues fanning themselves, takes several sips of their sodas to cool them down, and quietly continue with their beauty services, shaking their heads in disbelief of being blown away with a taste of Marque's reality and version of the birds and bees.

T' La June

Five - *Taken or Gay?*

"Ohhhh, ahhhhhh!" were the erotic sounds heard in the backseat of Cindy's darkened car. She comfortably laid alone, smiling with delight and content. She was again taking an intimate lunch break with her battery operated dildo, *Buzz Thick,* she treasured immensely. "Ahhh, ahhhh, ahhhhhhhh!" she quietly moaned with great pleasure as the hard, lubricated penis gently massaged and tingled her inner most private possession. "Oh, ohhh, ohhhhh shittttttt!" She moaned in a loud panting voice as her body climaxed with extreme explosions of gratification. The exhilarating buzzing toy was stimulating Cindy's sexual deprived enjoyments while she passionately savored in the pure happiness of its pleasure. Her body discharged a treasured moisture of satisfaction. "Ahhhhhh" she sighed with contentment after reaching her climax and coming back down to reality. "Who needs a real man when I have, *Buzz Thick,* my batteries a buzzin'." She teases as she cleans herself up, hides her dildo in the glove compartment, gets out her car, walks across the quiet parking lot, and goes back to work with a glow of contentment on her face and feelings of fulfillment that would last through the rest of the afternoon.

"Where have you been? You're late again." Tammy angrily uttered as Cindy walks into the office late from her lunch break.

Cindy quickly goes to retrieve a chart for a patient who has signed in and answers, "I'm sorry, I had a few runs to make and lost track of time." Cindy then thinks, "Yeah, and you wonder why I park so far away from the office. You just think I want the exercise. But what I really want is my private and undisturbed time with my toy." Cindy displays a devilish grin from her thought.

Tammy looks at her strangely, trying to figure out what Cindy's up to with the big smile on her face. "Maybe you should make your runs after work because you seem to come back from lunch late all

Not Quite Good Enough

the time now. Is there something I need to know?"

Smiling, Cindy answers, "Oh, no, everything is fine. I just lost track of time, that's all. I'll try harder to be on time in the future." Then she goes to the front of the office to call the patient into an examining room.

Tammy looks at her strangely, still wondering what's going on. Then she heads toward the room to see her patient. "Hi Mrs. Wells, how are you doing today?"

"I'm good Doctor Jones, and you?"

"I'm good too." Tammy checks Mrs.. Wells' blood pressure, and checks her chart for the cholesterol results. "Ok Mrs. Wells, you're fine. Your blood pressure and cholesterol look great. Keep doing what you're doing and you'll be just fine. I'll see you at your next appointment." Tammy tells the seventy-two year old elderly patient. She completes her checkup, in the upscale and classy medical office.

"Thank you Dr. Jones because I work very hard in trying to keep my health in good condition."

"Well, you're doing an excellent job, so keep up the good work."

"Thank you, I will. Now tell me Dr. Jones, during my last visit you told me you were looking for a good man. Did you ever find one? You're such a beautiful young lady."

"No, not yet. It seems a good man is hard to find." Tammy sadly acknowledges.

"Back in my days there were plenty of good men around."

"Mrs. Wells, I'm afraid that's not the situation nowadays. It seems that most of them are in jail, bums, or gay. Those are not the type of men I'm looking for."

"I surely understand. That's too bad." Mrs. Wells says.

"My feelings exactly, but what can you say." Tammy shakes her head. "Well, goodnight Mrs. Wells, that will be all for today. You're doing just fine since you changed your diet. Remember, stay away from all that sugar and salt so your levels will remain good. I don't want to have to put you back in the hospital. Continue to take care of yourself and don't let your medications run out on you again."

"Oh don't worry, I won't. I hate hospitals. I don't want to go to one anytime soon."

"That's good. Well, you're my last patient so I'll see you next month. I've got to get out of here so I don't miss my hair appointment. So now get dressed and go up front so Cindy can set up your next appointment. Have a good evening." Tammy hugs her patient and leaves the room.

Mrs. Wells smiles pleasantly, "Don't worry, I will."

As Tammy approaches the front office Cindy is talking on the telephone and has a medical record in her hand. Tammy gets her purse and jacket, and waves goodbye so she won't interrupt Cindy's conversation.

Mrs. Wells walks out the room before Tammy leaves, "Good luck honey in your quest, you'll find someone just for you. Just give it to God and let him take care of it. He'll find you a good man, mark my word. Our God is a mighty good God. Good night." Tammy smiles and agrees as she rushes out, leaving Mrs. Wells with Cindy.

Cindy makes Mrs. Wells' next appointment. "Here you go, you're all set for an appointment one month from today."

"Thank you dear."

"You're welcome. Have a wonderful evening." Cindy hands her an appointment card.

"I will and you do the same." Mrs. Wells walks toward the door to leave. Then she stops and turns back to Cindy, "Tell me young lady, are you also having a hard time finding a nice man?"

Surprised by her question Cindy blushes while feeling disappointed and answers, "Yes ma'am, I am. Why?" Cindy gains hope

Not Quite Good Enough

from the question and continues, "Do you know any good men?"

"Yes, kinda."

Cindy looks at Mrs. Wells and becomes pleasantly encouraged, "What do you mean kinda?"

Mrs. Wells explains, "Well, I have a nice son, Joe, who I think would be great for you. He's such a wonderful son. He makes sure I'm always taken care of. He calls me almost everyday to see how I'm doing. If he's not calling, he's over my house making sure I'm alright. The Lord God blessed me with a wonderful son, whom I love dearly. He's a hard worker and goes to school every night working toward his degree in engineering. He's going to make a girl very happy one day. I just hope it's not too soon."

Cindy looks at Mrs. Wells wondering what she's talking about. "What do you mean, you hope not too soon?"

Shaking her head in disappointment, Mrs. Wells explains herself. "Unfortunately he's taken right now. He's got some trifling young girlfriend he's dating now. I can't stand her, but he won't listen to a word I say, says he's in love. He tells me to stay out of his love life and let him handle things on his own. What can I say?" She throws up her hands and continues. "Maybe one day he'll wake up and smell the roses. I just hope he does it soon because I don't know how much longer I can put up with him seeing that little tramp. I truly believe she's the kind of girl who would get pregnant just to trap him, especially since she knows she has a good man. Then she would lie around the house, waiting for him to take care of her, hand and foot and not do a darn thing to help him. Lord God please forgive me for thinking like this, but I can't help the way I feel. I just believe that a mother always knows what's best for her kids, especially when it comes to love." Mrs. Wells' says in a disappointed tone and shakes her head.

Cindy smiles and with disappointment says, "Figures. All the good men are taken or they're gay. That's the kind a luck me and Tammy seem to have, but what can we say. We have to just keep looking."

"Yes you do child. Never give up on true love. Someone nice will come along soon. You ladies can't ever give up on your search for true love."

"We won't. But I sure hope that search hurries up because we're getting older." Cindy smirks.
"Trust me Child, I'm right."

Cindy shakes her head in disappointment and confesses, "I thought I had a special someone in my life several years ago, when I almost got engaged. But it didn't work out."

Mrs. Wells looks surprised and responds, "Really? Why? What happened?"

"Well, I thought Prince Charming had come into my life, but he was soooo corny and boring. He didn't even have a job. He didn't have time to party. He didn't drink. He was always studying for school. The only money he had was from financial aide, which he refused to spend on me. Bottom line, he just couldn't afford to take care of me, take me out, or buy me nice and expensive things like I wanted him to do. So, I couldn't see myself spending the rest of my life with him." Cindy explained.

Mrs. Wells is totally puzzled by Cindy's answer. "It sounds like he had great potential in being something really special, that's what's most important, his intentions."

Cindy continues to explain with a sparkling gleam in her eye, "Don't get me wrong, he was a great guy, and yes he had potential. But I wanted everything right then and right now! My friends thought I was crazy for not marrying him. He wanted to give me the world on a silver platter. He even kneeled down on one knee when he proposed to me with one of glass slippers he bought for me and told me that he

Not Quite Good Enough

was my Prince Charming, and I said NO." Cindy tears up at the thought.

Mrs. Wells is shocked and questions Cindy's reason. "Why did you say no? Because from what I've heard he seemed to really be a Prince Charming."

"Yes he was, he just wasn't MY Prince Charming." Tears fall down Cindy's cheek as she continues. "During that time I didn't think he was quite good enough for what I wanted in a man."

"So exactly what were you looking for?" Mrs. Wells asks and continues. "Because he sure sounds like he was definitely a keeper."

Embarrassed, Cindy answers to try and make it all make sense. "Deep inside I have to feel that the man I marry will be the exact man for me. I have to feel a certain connection with him and him with me. I have to know that we will be together forever. He has to be the man of my dreams, and unfortunately Prince Charming wasn't!"

Mrs. Wells begins to give Cindy words of wisdom. "Well Child, I hate to say it, but sometimes our Prince Charming is staring us right in our face. We don't always realize that until it's too late. Many people seek total perfection in a person right away, without giving them time to grow and develop. They don't accept a person who tries hard and loves you with everything they have, if what they have to give isn't perfect from the beginning. Relationships are, and should always be, works in progress, as long as BOTH parties are working toward perfection, because no one is flawless. People don't realize that they lost a good thing until it's long gone. I sure hope that's not what you did when you rejected his proposal."

Cindy is blown away from the wisdom of Mrs. Wells and admits, "Wow, I never thought of it like that, but you're right. He WAS the best thing that ever came into my life. But now it's too late. He married someone who USED to be my good friend. She simply told me, 'If you don't want him, I'll take him,' and take him she did with pleasure. He later graduated from college at the top of his class, got a great job, and began making a lot of money as a lawyer. They've been married now for over five years and have two beautiful children. He treats her like his princess. He worships the ground she walks on. She doesn't even have to work. Just think, that could have been MY life. But at the time, I didn't think he was good enough for me. Now he's gone! As I look back on that situation, I wish I would have been more understanding, extra patient, and less materialistic. I really blew that one! Now I can't seem to find a good man to save my life."

Mrs. Wells shakes her head, "Oh my, that's what I thought. Well, it's too late for him. Maybe God will give you another chance in finding true love. You're a nice young lady who just made a bad decision in finding true love. I just hope that now you are able to open your eyes to possibilities and don't let Prince Charming get away from you again."

Cindy has hope from Mrs. Wells words. "Believe me, the next time I spot Prince Charming, I'm definitely not going to make the same mistake! I just hope he hurries up and comes along, because I'm getting tired of waiting." Cindy says as she smiles and continues, "From your mouth to God's ears."

"Bless you child because God does answer prayers and he answers mine quite a bit. You see true love is very special. It only comes around once in a lifetime, and if you're lucky, or should I say, blessed, God may allow it to come around a second time. If you're lucky you'll find your soul-mate and live a long and happy life until you both die. I had a wonderful husband, Joe Sr., God rest his soul. We stayed together until the Lord called him home. Now that he's gone to be with our Lord, I'm all alone. However, I still feel blessed because we spent over fifty years together. Those memories will live with me until the day I die." Mrs. Wells shakes her head feeling happy and sad as she talks about her husband. "So, anytime I can help match-make

Not Quite Good Enough

a nice couple I do. I think everybody needs somebody nice in their life. Someone they can love forever. Someone who makes them smile. Just like my Joe used to do for me., God bless his soul." Mrs. Wells and Cindy have tears in their eyes as they smile and hug.

"I agree. Although, for me, Tammy, and a few of our friends, true love just doesn't seem to be found anywhere."

"Child, just be patient, your Prince Charming will come along again, just be patient. You and Doctor Jones are two beautiful and intelligent young ladies, so he'll eventually come. Keep asking God to grant you a good man and he will answer your prayer, but only when the time is right."

"Amen Mrs. Wells, Amen! I needed to hear that. I feel so much better now. I will do exactly what you said, continue to pray and wait. Although, once your son is available, please let me know. Because I'm sure he's a good man, just look at who raised him." Cindy smiles and hugs Mrs. Wells.

Feeling proud, Mrs. Wells beams and says, "Thanks baby, I will, I sure will. In the meantime, I'm gonna look out for you and Dr. Jones. I always find nice men around, they're normally the ones who help me when I'm in the grocery story, getting in my car, or helping me walk up the stairs." Mrs. Wells adds.

"At least someone is finding good men because we're sure not finding anyone good enough."

"He'll come when you least expect him to come sweetheart, just be patient and continue praying to God."

"I will and thank you Mrs. Wells. Have a wonderful evening."

"I will and you do the same." Mrs. Wells walks to the door and leaves, getting into a car where someone is waiting to drive her home.

"I will." Cindy closes and locks the door with new hope buried in her soul. As she turns off the lights and shut everything off

T' La June

in the office, she thinks with the reality of her sorrow, "Damn, all the talk about my Prince Charming has made me horny. I guess I'll be going home alone again, to another cold and lonely night shared with *Buzz Thick*. Oh well, a girl has got to do what a girl has got to do!" She then closes the back door, and walks to her car to go home.

Not Quite Good Enough

Six - *Thick Rich Chocolate Stick*

"Girl, you're late again! Get over here so we're not here all night long." Marque' scolds Tammy as she walks into beauty shop late for her appointment. He has just finished putting three bright new colors of hair dye on Mae May's hair. She waves at Tammy as she sits under the hair dryer.

Tammy hurries and takes her seat in Marque's chair. "I know I'm late, I'm sorry. But I ran behind with my appointments all day long."

"And what else is new? You're always late and then you want me to jump through hoops for you. Girl just sit down and let me do what I do because you're wayyy overdue, after missing your appointment two weeks ago." Marque' gets the scissors and begins taking out her weave and says, "Thank God you made it in this week because this head sure needs some TLC."

Tammy agrees, "I know it does and you know that's not how I do things. I gotta get a better handle on my schedule. I can't keep missing appointments. I have to do me, just like you have to do you! Anyway, I'm here now."

"Yeah you're here, but your ass better quit standing me up. I'm a popular bitch around here. I ain't got time to be waiting for your ass." They laugh. "Besides, you know you can't get your hair done as good as I can do it in that white neighborhood you work in. So just sit your ass back down and let me do my thang. Forget about all that proper shit. Now, how've you been?"

"I've been good, but before you start can you close the curtains? I don't want anyone seeing me get a weave."

"Why not? Bitch you weren't born with Indian hair. You was born with nigga hair like the rest of us and that's nothing to be ashamed of. So what you trying to hide?"

"Marque' you know people think this is all my hair. I don't want anyone to know the truth." Tammy says.

"Well, that's too damn bad bitch because I ain't closing the blinds. I might miss out on seeing a tight-ass honey walking by." They laugh as Marque' continues to cut the weave out of Tammy's hair.

"A new honey? Hell you've already slept with everyone around town who'll let you. So why are you still looking for new honeys? Besides, is getting a piece of ass all you ever think about?"

"Hell yeah! And that's all YOU should be thinking about, especially since you ain't had a dick in how long? Forever!" Tammy remains quiet and becomes embarrassed by his comment. "Hellooooo Miss high and mighty, I said, how long has it been since you've felt something hard, juicy, and wet in-between those long pretty brown legs of yours? Hellooo!" Marque' eyes Tammy with his hands on his hip waiting for an answer. "I don't hear anything? Hellooooo!"

"Don't talk so loud." Tammy says with embarrassment as she continues. "It's been awhile." She whispers.

Talking louder Marque' continues with the embarrassment, "What did you say? I didn't hear you."

She speaks a little louder, "Marque', quit talking so loud. I said it's been awhile."

"That's what I thought you said. But we're gonna change that shit real soon, even if I have to give you one of my bitches."
"Oh hell no! I won't ever be THAT desperate. Hellllll noooo!"

They laugh as Marque' continues, "Honey, first of all, lets keep it real. I know you want a man who has a lot of money. But bitch no matter how much money you make, you're still from the ghetto, and you still need to get your ass laid every once in awhile. The joy stick don't have to only come from a rich man. You see, poor brothas can screw just like rich ones, but they screw better because while they're not working hard making money, they're working hard making

Not Quite Good Enough

love. So, they've had more experience. In fact, the poor brothas are probably the best because they ain't got nothin' to lose but a hard joy stick, and everything to gain by laying that pipe right. And with the frequency of their experience, I'm sure Viagra is something few of them depend on." They laugh as he continues. "Besides, haven't you heard that it's a recession, so no damn body has a good job nowadays. Hell, if you got any kind of job you're doing good. So bitch quit being so damn choosy and stuck up, and get you some dick!"

Tammy responds, "That's one thing about you Marque', you always keep it real."

"Hell yeah I keep it real! And don't your ass ever forget that shit. Bitch, if I tell you the moon is made of cheese you better bring your crackers." they laugh. "So tell me, did you ever find Mr. Right or did you only find Mr. Right Now?"

"Hell no, I didn't find either of them!" She grins.

"Girl, with what you want in a man you ain't never gonna find Mr. Right. You better quit living in a damn fairytale and get real by finding a man who truly loves you, instead of a man who you only love for his money. Money can't keep you warm at night, nor can it make your coochie wet."

"Marque' I know you keep it real, but damnnnnnnn!" They crack up with laughter. "You're making it really real. I believe I'll find me a man soon. I know he's out there somewhere. So trust me, I'll find him."

"Yeah right. Tammy, not many brothas make the kind of money you want them to make. And finding a man who can give you that house with the so-called white picket fence around it, is some fairytale bullshit."

"Yeah I know it is, that's why I dip the white man's stick. I want that fairytale."

"But can that white man's dip stick, stick you like a brotha can?"

"Hell no! But don't worry, I'll always keep a brotha somewhere close by, even if I have to keep him hidden away in the closet," she confesses.

"Tammy if your ass did like I told you to do you'd have a cool brotha in your bedroom closet, to pull out for comfort anytime of the day or night you get horny. But you don't want to listen to me. I guess I don't know a damn thing, even though my bed is always HOT!" Marque' acts like he's blowing steam off his fingers and beams. "What? And go out with your broke ass friend?"

"You got that right, because from what I hear brotha man got it like that!"

"Oh hell no! I don't have time to be taking care of no grown ass man! Hell, he better be trying to buy me a filet mignon and lobster dinner, and not waiting for me to buy him one. I'm not the kinda sista who eats hamburger anything! You hear what I'm saying? I've worked too damn hard to settle for all that low-life shit!"

"Girlfriend, you're the one missing out. Brotha man can handle his business."

Tammy looks at Marque' with a strange look, "And just how do YOU know? Did you screw him too? I told you I'm definitely not interested in any of your leftovers."

"Believe me girlfriend, he ain't one of my leftovers and believe me when I say that I tried. He wasn't going for that shit. But all the sistas who've had a piece of him said he's worth the dip."

"Well, if I get desperate I'll give him a call. And who are you talking about anyway?"

"Sweets." Marque' answers.

"Sweets, oh hell no! That gigolo hoe. Hell, as many women as he's had he probably invented his own venereal disease."

Marque' defends his statement by saying, "Like I said, just dip the damn chocolate stick when you need to and move on. Hell, your g-spot ain't that damn good where you can't dip the stick of a healthy sized brotha! Shit, if he'd have me I'd dip, lick, and whip his thick rich chocolate stick all night long! Then I'd get up and make his cute ass some pancakes for breakfast and lick off all the maple syrup I'd spill on his silky thick body, lick by juicy slow lick." They laugh as Marque' makes sexual gestures with his tongue by sticking it out and rolling it around in circles.

Tammy shakes her head while laughing and said, "Like I said, it isn't anything wrong with dipping a brothas stick. Except, he should be more than thick and pretty. His ass should at least be able to take me out to a nice restaurant and feed me on his dime instead of mine. Dammit, I'm more than worth a good meal!"

"Tammy, from what I hear about dipping Sweet's stick is once you dip it, you'll be ready to pay his rent, car payment, and feed him strawberries and whipped cream by hand, like all his other hoes! Just ask Mae May." They laugh as Marque' walks to the hair dryer, knocks on the lid, and has Mae May come over and join in on the conversation.

"Damn, you scared my ass. I was having a good dream." Mae May fusses as she looks up at Marque'. "What you want?" "Shut up and come over here. Tammy needs to ask you a question."

Mae May walks to Tammy and sits in the chair next to her and Marque'. "Hey Tammy, What's up? What ya'll talking about that's so important that I had to get from under the dryer? My colors ain't locked in yet."

"Girl, forget about your hair. Tell Tammy about Sweets and his lovely dip stick. You know, the one you sampled and wanted to come back for more but he wouldn't let you." Marque' teases.

"Fuck you, you could have left off that last part of your smart-ass comment." They laugh as Mae May continues. "Anyway, girlllllllll!! That man! Damn, that man!" Mae May is smiling and shaking her

T' La June

head in pleasure as she attempts to explain. "Girl, I dipped his thick, chocolate brown, juicy stick one night after a few of us went to a club. This is how it went."

As Mae May begins to tell her story, she relives the night in full color, "Girl, we were in the club and it was dark as hell, filled with a lot of people who were dancing and drinking. The music was so loud you had to yell in order to hear someone talk. When all of a sudden, this FINE ass man walks in. I had never seen him before so I was really interested in who he was." Mae May smiles from ear to ear at the thought. "Hell, I didn't want to let him get away so I took my bold ass to the bar where he was standing and started talking to him."

Tammy is surprised by Mae May's admission. "You just walked up to him and you didn't even know him?" Tammy asks.

"Hell yeah! I got real bold that night. I figured I'd act the same way most men act when they want a woman, so I said; 'Damn, you look good enough to eat, what's your name?' He turned and looked at me and in a cocky tone, turned on his charm, 'They call me Sweet Daddy, but you can call me Sweets, Suga.' Then he pulls his sunglasses down past his eyes and smiles as he checks out my body. And believe me, I was looking good." Mae May gestures a silhouette shape of her body as she continues. "So of course I turned in a complete circle so he could get a good look and modeled my entire body. Girl, my dress was fitting so tight that night that you could see the g-string line that wrapped above my ass." Mae May laughs while jumping up and down with excitement.

"Damn, both of you sound like hoes." Tammy says as she looks at Mae May, and then at Marque' with them all laughing. "Go on." She encourages.

"Mae May is a hoe. I thought you already knew that." Marque' jokes.

"Fuck you Marque'," Mae May clowns around. "Shut up

and let me finish." She gives Marque' the evil eye and continues. "Then Sweets says, 'So, do you wanna see how many licks it takes to get to the center of my tootsie pop?' Girlllll, I was blushing from ear to ear after hearing that shit. So I figured since he was so bold I'd get just as bold. So I said, 'Hell yeah I wanna lick your tootsie pop and see what cums out. Then you can return the favor and see what cums out of my sweet jelly roll.' Girllllll, we were on a rollllll. I mean a tootsie-roll!" Everyone laughs at the story Mae May is telling as she rubs her hands together and boldly smiles with honor.

"Damnnnnn, you're too bold for me." Tammy says.

"I told you, you need to get with this brotha" Marque said to Tammy as Mae May continues.

"Girllll, after that, it was ONNNN!" Mae May delightfully teases and continues. "Next thing I knew we were butt naked in the back seat of his car getting it on! And damn was he good! It was so foggy in the car from our hot bodies rubbing together I could hardly see a thing. But seeing had nothing to do with anything because I could feel his thickness inside my body, as we worked our bodies out like we were training for a marathon! We rocked that car so hard that we set off the car alarms in the cars parked next to ours. Girl, he knew how to rock and roll his tootsie pop inside of my jelly roll so good that I exploded with sexual juices several times. In fact, the sex was so good, I could hardly keep up with his seductive ass and believe me, I can keep up with the best of the best." Everyone continues laughing.

In a sarcastic tone Tammy asks, while trying not to act like the description wasn't turning her on, "So what happened to you guys? Why aren't you together now if the sex was so damn good?"

"Tell her Mae May." Marque' encourages.

Mae May becomes depressed as she explains, "He didn't want me for more than just that night." Then she perks up. "Hell, if he'd take me I'd quit my job to be with that brotha just so he could screw my brains out every day and night. Like Tina Turner said, 'What's love got to do with a goddamn thang?'" Everyone laughs as Mae May dances erotically in circles.

Tammy desperately wanted to know more without seeming interested. "What happened after all this so-called good sex? I know you didn't throw in the towel that easy, or did you?"

"After we came up for air we started talking and smoking a cigarette. He said he needed to be taken care of financially. I told him I had four kids to take care of and taking care of a man didn't fit in my budget."

"Go on, don't stop there. Tell the rest. We're listening." Marque' encourages as Mae May continues.

Mae May cuts her eyes at Marque' with a bitter look and continues. "After that, he told me that even though the sex was good, it would never work between us. He said I wasn't his type, had too many babies, and I couldn't afford him. He said every woman he's with has to pay his cost, so that he can be their boss. He said, he only gave me a sample of his love so I'd pay for it later. Then he told me that he was afraid that my three inch nails would scratch out his eyes, scar his face, and ruin his pretty boy image, which was a chance he wasn't willing to take."

"He said all that?" Tammy questions.

Embarrassed, Mae May answers, "I think he was just trying to let me down easy."

"Does this man even have a real job?" Tammy questions again.

"No, not really. Unless you call his being a male hoe, having a real job."

Tammy is upset by what she's hearing. "He's got his damn nerves. At least you have a real job and take care of your kids. But wait, you said you have four kids? Where's their daddy? Does he help you?"

Not Quite Good Enough

"Well, my momma keeps them for me while I work. And no, my babies daddies don't take care of them. All of their daddies are either in jail or on drugs. Besides, I don't need their no-good asses anyway. I get welfare assistance and they pay my mom to keep the kids for me. So I don't need their money. These days, all I need a man for, is for a piece of dick when I get horny."

"Which is every day." Marque' adds.

"Listen to who's talking." Mae May blasts Marque' "Shut up and let me finish." She says and continues. "Since I have help from the county, I don't need none of my babies no-good, piece of shit, ass daddies anyway. Besides, I've gotten better assistance from the county than I've ever gotten from a man." Mae May becomes quiet and holds her head down in embarrassment.

Marque feels bad for Mae May and adds, "Ain't nothing wrong with a little public assistance when you need it. But as far as those kids of yours, my God-babies, all I got to say is their asses are baddd!" He jokes. "So I don't blame Sweets or any other man for not wanting to be bothered. Hell, if I liked women I wouldn't even touch you if I knew you had all those bad ass kids. Their bad asses would turn any good or bad man away from you." He and Tammy laugh. Mae May laughs and fires back, "Fuck you Marque'"

"Maybe if you didn't tell the men you date you had four kids, or if they didn't meet their bad asses, you could get and keep a man!"

Tammy is laughing hard, almost falling out her chair. "Wait, waitttt, just how many babies daddies do you have?"

"Four." Mae May responds.

Tammy shakes her head in disbelief, "Damn girl, are you serious?"

"Seeeee, I told you she's a hoe." Marque' joins in.

Mae May defends herself. "That's cold, shut up already! You guys are crazy." She puts her hand high in Marque's face, as to shut him up and turns to Tammy. "As I was saying, girl, Sweets dip stick is so good he doesn't need a job. Dipping that stick the way he does is why so many women take care of his cute ass. I'm surprised he hasn't chased after you yet. You got money, and he's definitely attracted to any woman with money, especially if she's as cute as you are. You could definitely be someone who could take care of his needs and him return the favor."

"I met the brotha awhile ago. He chases me every time he sees me. But I don't give him the time of my day. Hell, I don't have any time for a broke ass, gigolo hoe like Sweets. He is definitely someone beneath my level. He is definitely not good enough for ME!" Tammy holds her nose high in the sky.

"There you go getting all prissy on us again." Marque' points out. "Girl, from what I hear that man will make you lose your religion, let alone your sense of pride, after a taste of his tootsie roll. If I were you, I'd put away my stuck up pride and double dip his hot, chocolate, juicy stick anytime he gave it to me. Hell, who has pride when you can have a taste of something good and plenty." Marque' grins and gives Mae May a high five.

"Like I said, I don't have time to take care of any man. What I need is a real man with a real job, not a gigolo hoe who's only good for a good screw." Tammy fires back.

"Well you're the one going around saying how much you want a man, not me. I have plenty and I'm not sharing any of mine. So don't say I didn't warn you when you need a damn navigational system just to find your g-spot, or when your jelly roll dry's up so hard you need to buy a new jar of K-Y jelly just to lubricate it. Girl, you need to forget about who has money and just get that dip stick and get to licking! From what I've heard, it'll leave you smiling from ear to ear. Just like the one I have who leaves me smiling every night!"

"Well, just any dip stick isn't quite good enough for me, I need more." Tammy demands.

Not Quite Good Enough

"Good luck in finding him. Until then, I'll be getting mine and while I'm at it I'll make sure to get some for you too." Marque' teases Tammy.

Mae May throws up her hands, "Lord have mercy, I'll be getting mine too! That's how I got four kids by four different daddies in the first place! And hell, if the stick is as good as Mr. Sweet Daddy's is, then, I'll just have to work on daddy number five!" They laugh as Marque' finishes Tammy's hair and Mae May goes back to the hair dryer.

T' La June

Seven - *I Want Some Dick Too*

"Hey girl, did you get some dick last night like you were hoping for?" Vicki teased Sophia while talking to her on the phone.

"No, and believe me I tried." Sophia embarrassedly jokes. "Then a drunken jerk bought me a drink and thought I owed him sex for his kindness, the asshole."

Vicki falls out, howling with laughter. "I don't know why you try so hard to get a man. They only make you feel like you're not worth anything. Hell, you can do bad all by yourself." Suddenly Vicki's tone becomes serious as she continues. "If you let me, I can make you feel better than any man you've ever been with."

"Vicki, you know I don't roll like that anymore, I like me some dick, but thanks for the offer. If that's what YOU want to do, do what you got to do, but leave me out of this one. You would think a 37 year old woman would be able to get a good man by now. I know I'm not the skinniest woman out there, but I am a good person. So why can't I get a good man? I'm trying really hard but it still isn't working. I seem to only be good enough to be someone's friend, or be someone's booty call. I'm never the girl a man wants to take home to meet their mom. Hell, I want some dick just like other women do. Besides, everybody needs somebody, so why can't someone need me?" Sophia feels sorry for herself, dropping a few tears at the thought.

Vicki is not feeling sorry for Sophia at all and insists on teasing her. "Girl, you're killing me with all that feeling sorry for yourself bullshit. You'll get someone if that's what you really want. Just go on with your life and buy you a new vibrator until you find someone. At least if you have a vibrator, you won't forget what it feels like to be turned on or to get your coochie wet." she laughs and continues. "Then, when Mr. Right does comes along you'll be good and ready. You don't want your coochie to be all dried up like it was a part of a 37 year drought!"

Not Quite Good Enough

Vicki teases.

"Vicki quit making fun of me. You know you want a man too."

"Not really. If I find one that's cool, but I'm not going to chase after just anybody's joy stick. Hell, I'm better than that. I'm an educated woman with a damn good job. I don't need a man to justify who I am or take care of me. I can do that on my own." Vicki admits.

"I guess that means your vibrator is working just fine," Sophia claims. "But one things from sure, your fancy college degree can't keep you warm at night."

"Although, my hand, electric blanket, and a great vibrator do work very well together when I need them to." Vicki again teases.

"It's times like these when only a straight woman understands my pain and that's definitely NOT you. Right now I'm not trying to go back to that gay lifestyle. That was happening during my crazy college days. Nowadays, I want and need a good man. I want to feel satisfied when he holds my hand, kisses my lips, and takes me in his arms to make love to me. That's what I want."

"Girlll, I hear what you're saying. A girl has to do what a girl has to do. As for me, the jury is still out. On that note, I'm getting off the phone. I'm horny as hell right now with all this talk about men and dicks. I just bought some new batteries, so I'm ready for some fun and excitement."

"You're nuts." Sophia teases.

"Until you do get a man, take it from me and get you a few new batteries to make you feel warm and fuzzy inside."

"Girl, you're crazy. I don't know about you sometimes."

"I sure am crazy, crazy about taking care of my own damn business and not relying on anyone to make me feel good." Vicki jokes and continues, "Anyway, I'll talk to you tomorrow. Hang in there." The sound of a vibrator is heard in the background before Sophia can hang up the phone and she laughs.

"Vicki you're crazy. But it's all good. I'll find a man even if it means putting an ad in the newspapers. Goodnight."

"And you call me crazy. Goodnight." They laugh as they hang up the phone and go to bed alone, fulfilling their needs in different ways.

As they hang up their phones, Sophia turns up her television, and grabs a bag of chips and a soda to keep her company.

Not Quite Good Enough

Eight - *Gigolo Hoe*

Cindy is in the office getting the day started when Tammy walks in. "Girl, your hair looks good. Marque' can do some hair." Cindy turns Tammy in a complete circle so she can see the entire hairstyle. "I can't wait for him to do mine tonight."

"He sure can do some hair with his ghetto ass gay self." They laugh as Tammy looks at her mail.

"Ghetto and gay, that's definitely Marque'. But what trips me out is that he has some good looking men chasing after his cute ass. The worse part of that story is that most of the men who come in the shop to see him don't look gay." Cindy adds, "Just think, we can't get one straight man, let alone have a choice to pick from like Marque'. Something's definitely wrong with that picture. Hell, we need to discover his secret. Maybe then we can get a good man!" They laugh.

"His secret is he's a male hoe!" Tammy jokes. "Marque' will do anything to and for a gay man; anyway or anyhow they want him to do. In the meantime he's enjoying every bit of his pleasure, no matter how many men want to screw him. Even if it means screwing several at the same time. So, if you want to be a hoe, I'm sure you'll find plenty of men and women to participate with you. Although you won't find a good one that way. But hey, I guess the good side of it all is that you'll have a ton to choose from since so many people are all about the sex nowadays. Then, at the end of the day you may feel content, or you may not, but will it be worth it? One thing is for sure is that you'll definitely get your freak on!" They laugh as Tammy dances the booty dance.

"Well, if being a hoe gets you plenty of men then I need to get busy, because I'm tired of being lonely and horny. Hell, my coochie feels as dry as the Grand Canyon right about now and I hate the wilderness." Cindy said as they laugh.

"Girl don't be silly by settling for less than you deserve. Hell, we deserve good men who have good jobs, that can take care of us. We want the ones who can wine and dine us every night, if we want, at a five star restaurant. At least I know I deserve the best, because I ain't cooking for no man." Tammy brags.

"I agree, but where are they? Tammy it's been a few years since I've had a good man and I let him get away because he didn't have a good job."

"Like I said, you deserve better."

"That's what I keep telling myself. But that doesn't keep me warm at night. Besides, listening to Marque' talk about all the men he's been with and what they do to him makes me so horny that I have to run home and change my panties after I leave his shop, because they are wet as hell."

Tammy looks at Cindy weird, "Damn girl, you really do need a man. But all Marque' will do is hook you up with Sweets, the gigolo hoe. That way he can enjoy listening to your screwing adventures since Sweets won't screw him."

"Yeah, I heard about Sweets and his personal home delivery service. But girl I'm so desperate right now I just may have to give Mr. Sweetness a call one night. Things are getting a little too dry down south for me. Hell, I need the natural lubrication of a man every once in awhile and right now I'm wayyyyy overdue." Cindy jokes. Cindy pulls out Sweets' business card and shows to Tammy. "Girl, don't he look good enough to eat? Here, I got one for you too." Cindy smiles as she gives Tammy a card.

Tammy looks at the card and frowns. She then lays it back on the desk teasing Cindy. "Girl you're crazy. I don't want this card, he sure ain't good enough for me. You keep it." Tammy begins to walk away. "We better get to work before a patient comes in and hears us talking like we're two desperate dogs in heat." They laugh. "But we are." Cindy jokes as they get back to work and a patient walks into the office.

Not Quite Good Enough

Nine - *Naked and Hot!*

Cindy arrives for her nail and hair appointment. "Hey girl, sit in my chair. I'll be right with you. I gotta pee real bad." Mae May tells Cindy while running to the restroom.

"Ok. Hey everybody." Cindy says while waving at everyone in the beauty show and sitting down at Mae May's manicure station.

"Hey Cindy, I'm almost done with Sophia. I'll do your hair after Mae May finishes your nails." Marque' said.

"Ok." She answers and grabs a magazine to read while waiting.

After a few minutes, Mae May returns, "Whew, I've been holding that one for a longgggggg time!" Mae May said as she sits down to do Cindy's nails. "I feel better now. So, what you been up too girl?"

"Just working and still trying to find a good man."

"Girl, who don't want a good man. I for damn sure want one. So, when you find one, let me know if he has a brother or uncle."

"I heard that." Cindy agrees as they laugh.

Marque' adds his two cents, "Mae May, the only way you're gonna find a good man is if he doesn't know you have four bad ass kids at home and if you cut down those long ass fingernails." Cindy laughs.

Mae May rolls her eyes at Marque' and looks at Cindy like she's crazy. "Excuseeeeeeeeee Meeeeccccc, 'Miss I'm STILL looking for a man.' You got your damn nerve laughing and Marque' mind your own business. Marque', you think you know what you're talking about. But you don't know a damn thing about why I can't get a man, so shut the hell up." Cindy can't help but to cackle up with laughter as the battle continues.

Marque' takes a double look at Mae May and prepares to defend himself, "Shut up? Who me, shut up? Oh hellll to the nawww bitch!" he sarcastically jokes. "Girl, don't no man want a woman with nails that damn long where you can barely wipe your ass, let alone wipe his if he needed you to do so."

"Damnnnnn Marque', that's coldddddd!" Cindy instigates.

"Mae May, you also need to tone down a few of those bright ass colors in your hair. What is it now, four or five? Hell, it's all starting to blend together and look like a damn maze up in your head. So, unless Mr. Right is looking for Mrs. Clown, tone that shit down now!" Marque' teases as everyone laughs.

"Marque' now, that's cold." Mae May attempts to make him feel bad. "I thought I was your best friend. Besides, you're the one who dyed my hair in the first place and told me I looked good. So now you wanna diss my hair and nails like they ain't the shit when I know they're tha bomb." Mae May holds her hands high in the air, proudly displaying her multi-color studded artwork and fluffs out her hair as she continues the battle. "Well brotha, I got something for your black ass. See, you can't talk because your hair looks like a tall gold ass statue sitting on top of your head like a forth of July firework display filled with glitter, or one of those damn spot lights trying to attract people to their business." Everyone laughs at the cracks about Marque'.

Marque' strikes a pose, getting his ammunition ready for war. "Oh hellllll to the naaaahhhhh Sista!" He continues, "Don't start with me with your ghetto ass, man chasing, baby momma drama, hoe-ish ass." he flares with humor. "Girl you better recognize who gets all the big and thick joy sticks around here and it ain't you! Snap!" Everyone is laughing so hard that some are falling out their chairs while the battle between Marque' and Mae May carries on.

Mae May is laughing and shaking her head. She can't get a word in because Marque' is on a roll of winning his battle. "Hell, I taught you everything you'll ever know about hair, nails, and joy sticks. So little Sista, get it straight who the original diva is around here, and watch what ya saying. Besides, my gold hair is a high class fashion statement. So recognize that gold is in and all those damn colors you got in your hair is wayyyy the hell out of style! Heyyyyyyy!" Marque' snaps his fingers high in the air, twists his body, and continues doing his clients hair while Mae May and everyone laugh.

"Well Mr. Smarty-ass pants," Mae May strikes back, "For your information, I can wipe my ass just fine, and my man's ass too if needed, thank you very much! As for my colorful hair, it's MY fashion statement and no one else's because I'm an original diva." She points to herself as she proves her point. "It gets me all the attention I want. It also gets me all the dick I want, when I want it." She fires back and does a dance by shaking her butt and bouncing around in circles.

"It sure as hell does get you attention, but the wrong kind." Marque' jokingly adds before getting serious. "But on the real Mae May, you know you're my boo girl. I love you like you were my blood sister. That's why I'm telling you the truth." Marque' runs over to Mae May and hugs her before returning back to his station to continue his battle. "But really girl, have you looked at yourself in the mirror lately? If you ask me, you need to get a make-over and take some of those damn colors out your hair. Last night you left out of here with three colors now you got, how many, five? Damnnnn girl! Let's take some time to clean you up so you really can get a man. Maybe then you'll stop all that damn complaining you've been doing for years, and get you a joy stick that will STAY in your bed instead of playing musical beds!" Everyone laughs.

"I don't remember asking for your advice Mr. Think-he-knows-it-all! My looks are just fine." Mae May sticks her tongue out at Marque' and laughs with everyone in the shop, as she continues doing Cindy's nails.

"All I gotta say is when you do get a man, get one for me too, because I for damn sure need one." Sophia adds.

"Sophia, I thought you had a man since we haven't seen you around here in awhile."

"Mae May, that's why I'm back. I need a make-over and nobody does hair and makeup as good as Marque'." Marque' sticks out his tongue to Mae May as Sophia continues. "I figure some waxing on my arms, legs, eyebrows, lips and chest will help. Then with a facial, pedicure, acrylics, and a new hairstyle will at least get someone to pay me more attention. Besides, I'm tired of guys always thinking of me as their friend or sister, and not their girlfriend or lover. I want a joy stick up in this dry coochie too! Shit, my coochie is so dry that when I walk, tumbleweeds roll down my legs." Everyone laughs, falling out their chairs as Sophia continues.

"Hell, it's so dry that it has cobwebs growing inside. The worse part about that is it's so dry that even the spiders are crawling down my legs once they get in looking for some kind of moisture besides my daily showers. They crawl up in there and when they can't find any air they run the hell back out." Mae May falls out her chair and howling with laughter. Everyone laughs at her reaction and joins in.

"Well, if you damn bitches would just listen to me you'd have a joy stick inside those dry coochies. Hell, I can't suck em' all, even though I try to!" Marque' smiles, then opens his mouth wide and licks his lips in circles while everyone is laughing.

"Marque' that's the problem right there, we can't get a man because you have 'em all."

"Sophia, don't be a hater! Be a lover! Or better yet a sucker!" They laugh as he finishes Sophia's hair, gets ready for Cindy and continues. "In fact, you bitches need to call Sweets because from what I've heard HE'S the man around town, just ask Mae May."

Mae May closes her eyes, sticks out her tongue, and rotates it around her thick lips. She slowly positions her finger inside her mouth and gently massages it with passion from the warm juices buried deep within. Then she gently releases her finger out while ending the motion of pleasure with a loud, juicy smack. "Does THAT explain how good Sweets was with me ya'll!" She brags as the reactions from everyone in the shop is dripping with envy and desire.

"Damnnnnn, where's his number and how come you're not with him now?" Cindy boldly asks.

"Girl, it's a long story and right now I can't get into it."

"Why? Because I want to hear this story as well." Sophia asks.

"My hormones are too sensitive right now and if I tell you, I'll start crying." Mae May sadly acknowledges and goes back to working.

"Yeah, her damn hormones are sensitive my ass." Marque' fires back with humor. "The real story is that the brotha didn't want to have anything to do with her ass after he found out she has four kids and couldn't pay his bills. Hell, she ain't been the same ever since. Now Mae May, say I'm lying." Everyone looks at Mae May, who never looks up as he proceeds. "But that's alright, she'll snap out of her funk soon. She can't go too long without a joy stick, trust me, I know her." Everyone laughs, even Mae May, but she continues to keep her silence.

Everyone is shocked by her silence so Cindy comments. "Damn, I guess he was really good and broke your heart. She still ain't saying a word to defend herself and normally she's ready to talk smack with you Marque'" Cindy said.

"See, I told you. But she'll be alright, won't you Mae May?" Marque' gives her serious look as he waits for her answer.

"Yeah, yeah, yeah! I'm fine, so get off the subject and talk about something else." Mae May sarcastically reacts.

"I will after I tell them a little more." Marque' goes on with his story, instigating Mae May to defend herself. "Ladies, from what

T' La June

Mae May and a whole lot of other women have told me, you see I have to rely on a woman's word. Sweets won't let me discover his world for myself; nor will he let any other man taste his good and plenty joy stick." Everyone laughs. "But everyone says he's the real deal in bed. Wait, check this out!" Marque' stops and goes to the front of the store and grabs a few business cards out of a fancy leather holder. "Check these out," he passes the cards around to every woman in the shop and continues. "Sweet's is so serious that he has his own business cards. He passes them out to anyone who thinks they can afford him. Now, tell me this isn't a real businessman doing shit like this."

Once the ladies have the colorful glossy business card in their hands their mouths immediately open wide as they observe the naked male body, with caramel colored skin, and displaying a muscular flexed six pack chest; laying on his side revealing his entire upper body, posing on a fluffy white sheep skin rug, while holding his head up high in his hand. He's flexing a super fine arm of powerful oily muscles, while wearing only a white cowboy hat and a smile. His naked and revealing body vanishes just inches below his muscular waistline. "Damnnnnn, look at that body." Cindy says with excitement. She continues, "This card is making me hot!" She begins fanning herself with a nearby magazine. "It's even making my panties wet, the same way singer D'Angelo makes me feel every time I watch his 'How Do You Feel' video." She grins.

"Double damnnnn girl, but I know what you mean!" Sophia adds with a big smile on her face, also reaching for a nearby magazine to fan herself from all the excitement.

"I told you ladies that Sweets is a serious businessman. Just look, his prices are listed on the back." When they turn the card to the back, it displays a bright and colorful picture of his long caramel muscular legs, one bent upwards, and the other lays down flat. His

Not Quite Good Enough

feet feature a highly expensive pair of black shiny cowboy boots. "Triple damn!" Sophia adds as her mouth waters with excitement.

"I knew you ladies would enjoy the view." Marque' adds with a big grin on his face. "He keeps his cards fully stocked in the shop because they disappear regularly."

"I can see why they disappear." Cindy adds.

Marque continues, "See, this man's real job is for women to take care of him while in turn he takes care of them." Marque' blushes and also grabs a magazine to fan himself from the excitement. "Every time I look at this card I get mad he ain't gay. Damn, damn, damnnnnnn!" He jokes as the women laugh and fan themselves from their hot flashes.

"Look at what the card says," Cindy begins reading the top. "Let me be your Good and Plenty 'SWEETS' 555-4398." Then she fans more. "Damnnnn! He for damn sure can be mine anytime. However, from the look of these prices I can't afford to play anything with him. But I'll keep the card just in case I hit the lottery or something." She jokes as everyone laughs.

"I heard that, me too." Sophia adds as she reads the bottom of the card, "You can be MY 'Suga Baby' tonight!" Damnnnn! I'm keeping this card forever! Hell, I'm framing mine." Everyone laughs as Sophia again fans herself.

"I'm keeping mine too." Cindy joins in. "And give me one for Tammy, just in case she gets desperate. She's the only one around here that can afford his prices."

Marque' gives her another card. "That bitch ain't ever gonna be THAT desperate to pay for the services of a man like Sweets." Marque' said. "She's too damn stuck up to ever do anything like that, so don't even waste your time." He gets ready to take back the card.

Cindy stops him. "Wait, don't take it. I'm still gonna give it to her, especially since I can't afford him. Maybe she'll treat me for a ride on this cowboy as a work bonus one day. Shittt, for the price of him, I'll give up my yearly raise. Yeee Haaa!" Cindy clowns around as everyone laughs.

"Well, if that happens I wanna hear all about it, detail by dripping detail." Marque' adds with lustful intentions.

"Yeah, me too." Sophia joins in. "In fact, I need to start a Christmas fund just to treat myself for a ride on Sweets. Forget about buying other people a Christmas gift. Hell, I'll treat myself to a gift just to spend a night with Mr. Good and Plenty. That way I'll be buying myself something that will last everyday I think of him, and also in my dreams. Spending a night with him would definitely put a smile on my face." They laugh. "Awwww damnnnnn! He looks good and his body, damnnnn, no words can describe how good his body looks!" Sophia shakes her head in disbelief, indicating that Sweets is too good to be true. "In fact, he looks good enough to eat for breakfast, lunch and dinner. I just can't say it enough damn, damn, damnnnnn!" Everyone again laughs.

"Ok hot momma, I'm done with you." Marque' said to Sophia as he takes off her cape. Everyone is laughing as she gets out of his chair. "You can go to the restroom now and dry off. After all this talk of sleeping with Sweets, I know your coochie is dripping wet. I for damn sure am dripping buckets." Marque' confesses as he quickly walks to the mens restroom. "I'll see you in two weeks."

"Ok, I'll see you then." Sophia blushes while running to the women's restroom.

A few minutes later, Sophia and Marque' come out their restroom's. Marque' says, "Sophia, before you leave, get your invitation and give one to Vicki."
Sophia asks, "What invitation? What's going on?"
"Yeah, what invitation?" Cindy said.
Marque' jokes; "If you crazy bitches were paying attention

Not Quite Good Enough

you would have noticed the big ass sign on the wall when you walked in advertising our annual Valentine's Day party. This year we're inviting five other salons to join us at a fancy downtown hotel. It's gonna be big!"

"Well, excuse the hell out of me." Sophia jokes as she looks across the room and sees the sign. "I guess I didn't notice your big ass sign." she laughs. "Give me my invitation now. I need to go to a good party, you guys always throw good parties with lots of single men. I'm sure with the extra salons coming, there should be plenty of men to choose from."

"Yeah, but remember Sophia, lots of single men doesn't mean they're all straight men." Cindy looks at Marque', smiles and continues. "Marque', can you please tell YOUR friends to let us ladies know if they're gay or straight BEFORE we start claiming them?" Cindy teases as everyone agrees.

Marque' shakes his head and says, "See, that's ya'll's problem. You can't tell a good man from a really good man, if you catch my drift!" Marque' raises his eyes and bats his lashes. "None of them are ever good enough for ya'll's asses." he teases more. "Anyway, both of you get an invitation and give one to your girls Vicki and Tammy. Each invitation has four invite cards that you can give to a friend or family member. Mark my words, this is going to be a kick-ass celebration, heyyyy! "Marque' raises his hands in the air and snaps his fingers while everyone laughs and joins in. "Heyyyyyyyyy!!!"

"Count me in. Me too!" Cindy and Sophia add.

"Don't forget to bring your own damn drink." Marque' insists. "Cause we ain't providing any booze. We'd go out of business if we tried to serve all these lushes that we have as customers." he teases. "This party is strictly for each salon's customers and their close friends and family. So don't invite everyone you know; only those who are special. It's gonna be off the chain! Heyyy." Marque' said as everyone again joins in. "Heyyyyyy!"

T' La June

Ten - *The Climax*

It's late in the evening when a loud knock is heard at the door of Tammy's high rise apartment building. The intense sound surprises her, causing her to become afraid, "Oh my God, who's banging on my door like that?" she thinks and quickly runs to the door to look out the peephole. She sees a police officer's uniform but is unable to determine whether it's a man or woman. The officer's head is positioned toward the floor, only revealing the top of the hat and the uniform. Tammy wonders, "Why is a policeman at my door?" Suddenly the knock gets louder, causing her to become intimidated. Tammy yells while trying to not show her fear. "Who is it?" She begins to shake.

No voice is heard, only the knocks get louder and louder, scaring her even more. "I said who is it?" she yells with fear.
The policeman responds, "I'm looking for a Ms. Tammy Jones."

Puzzled and afraid, she slowly opens door, leaving the chain still attached she peeks out. "Yes, may I help you?"

The policeman lifts up his head, looks directly into Tammy's eyes and licks his lips. He smiles and begins dancing in an erotic style. Tammy beams with pleasure after realizing its Sweets, unchains the door, grabs his tie, and quickly pulls him inside. "You scared me."

Sweets begins kissing her, "Suga' I don't want to scare ya, I just want to make love to ya." He dances sexy for her as he strips naked, with her rubbing his chest. Tammy is pleasantly admiring every peck of his powerful and muscular six pack.

Earlier that evening, and out of desperation, Tammy broke down, located Sweets' telephone number, and made the desperate call to have Sweets personally service her overdue sexual needs. Not sure if he could make a service call with such short notice, Tammy was not expecting his well received and unexpected visit. After walking into Tammy's upscale condo, ready for love, Sweets wraps his

Not Quite Good Enough

muscular arms around her tiny body and massages it next to his with great passion.

Tammy enjoys the gesture and responds, "Ummm, I've been waiting for you." she moans as he kisses her neck.

"Well, wait no more because Sweet daddy is here and I'm gonna serve you good and plenty tonight." He kisses her, reaching his tongue in areas she forgot she had.

She returns the intense passion as they walk, lip to lip, down the hallway to her bedroom, while he grabs a hold of her behind, carefully fondling it with a delicate grip. With all the talk in the beauty shop about Sweets, and how he could please a lady, Tammy was ready for his pleasure.

"Ummm, it's been far too long." Tammy passionately kisses him all over his body while he undresses her out of her sexy white laced baby-doll lingerie.

While deep in the moment of their passion, Sweets caresses her breast with his mouth, slowly tasting the tenderness of her body with his tongue. Tammy closes her eyes and enjoys the feel of her nipples being stroked between the deep layers of his warm and soft lips.

Sweets is breathing deeply, enjoying Tammy's reaction. "Damn girl, I know you want me, but slow down. I'm not going anywhere anytime soon. Let's relax and take our time."

During this time, is when little sweet and innocent Tammy was gone out the window, leaving the tiger in her roaring out for more. "I've haven't had sex in almost a year, I don't have time to slow down. I need you inside me now!" she demands.

Sweets begins to deliver Tammy's sexual needs by gently inserting his well-endowed, hardened manhood into her most intimate and private possession, as she passionately screams with pleasure and satisfaction. "Yes, yes, yessss!" she moans with enchantment.

T' La June

The more he rocks her world, the more she wants him inside her body, "Moreeee, oh I want you moreeeeee!" While having sex, Tammy is sweating like she's doing a daily work out in an aerobics class at high speed. She continues to intensely scream, "Sweetsssssss! Yes, Sweets, yesssss!!! You make me feel sooo damn gooddddd! Yessss!" She yells with desire.

As the passion heats up to higher levels, Sweets' lips began to passionately travel to her neck, where her head leans backward, as if it was touching her back, while she enjoys the soft and moist touches his lips offers. His lips then descend down to her breast, where he slowly savors each nipple, one at a time, in the comfort of his warm mouth, creating an elevated delight.

Shortly after, he begins tasting the moisture on her warm body as it gravitates to her navel, allowing his tongue to gently circulate around its creation with passion. Just when Tammy thought his pleasures couldn't get any better, he reaches for her legs, spreading them far apart. His head then vanishes deep inside, where his tongue plunges in search of forgotten treasures hidden in-between her inner thighs. As he savors the taste of her most precious juices, she moans with intensity, "Damn Sweets, you make me feel soooo damnnnn gooddddd! Please don't stop!" Tammy screams with desire and enjoyment.

Since growing up in the same hometown, being a former girlfriend, and her first love, Sweets and Tammy have been away from each other for years. So it's been a long time since they've had sex. For Tammy, the sex is so good she yells out. "Sweets, please don't stop! Noooo Sweets, don't stop!!! You feel sooooo damn good inside of me! Please Sweets, don't stopppp!" Each time his name is called, Sweets wants to hear it again, "Who's your daddy bitch? Who's your daddy?"

"You are Sweets, you are my daddy, baby!" she intensely

Not Quite Good Enough

answers, "Oh, Sweetsssssss!"

The intensity of the sex is so strong it rocks her bed, causing the bedpost to crash and bang against the wall. The strong force of the banging bedpost causes the sex to get even wilder with him grasping on to her hips with great need as he rides her like she's his pony.

"Yes, yes, yessss!" She shouts. "Oh my, this feels soooo damnn goodddd!" she declares. Her body reaches heights she hasn't reached in years. "Yes, oh yessss!" she screams with her eyes closed, while enjoying total gratification.

Suddenly, Sweets picks her up, wrapping her in his muscular arms, and carries her to the kitchen. He places her naked body on the counter-top, stands in-between her gapped legs, aims them toward the ceiling, while positioning them in a V, for victory. He then feels her up with his passion like she's never felt before. "Uhhhhhh, uhhhhhh! This feels sooo damnnnn goodddd!" she yells with excitement, while her closed eyes reveal true sexual fulfillment. He once again passionately rocks her world.

As the sex heats up even more Sweets suddenly stops; "Oh shit, get up, my condom came off." He searches for his lost condom.

Tammy panics and pushes him away. "Damn Sweets, where is it? You can't be doing that shit, I'm not on any birth control!" Sweets continues looking for the condom, "Why the hell not?"

"Because I haven't been screwing anyone in almost a year. Why do you think I called you? Here it is, it's inside of me." She pulls the condom out of her vagina and throws it at him. "Damnnnnn. I hope I don't get pregnant because I'm super fertile right now."

"I hope you don't either because I don't want any more kids. Do you want me to stop?"

"Hell No!" she says with lustful eyes, "But this time make sure your condom stays on."

"Your wish is my command." Sweets again picks Tammy up,

carrying her to the living room couch while they passionately kiss. He puts on another condom as they continue their sexual feelings. Tammy is enjoying every moment of her fiery hunger while making loud moaning sounds. "Ahhhhhhhh, ohhhhhhhhhh, ahhhhhhhhh!!!"

Suddenly she screams as she climaxes. Her body begins to shake as she cries with intensity. "Oh shit I'm cummingggg!!! Oh shitttttt!!! Yes, yes, Yesssssss!!!"

Sweets is enjoying the moment and encourages her, "Cum on baby, that's it, cum on for Sweet daddy! Oh shit, Sweet daddy is cumming too! Oh shittttt! Goddamn girl!"

Riding each other like there is no tomorrow, Tammy brings her passion home. "That's it! Oh baby, that's itttttt!!! Oh babyyyyyy!!!!" She yells with more emotion.

"Call my name Bitch, call my nameee!" Sweets aggressively demands while rocking her world.

As her body peaks to its most extreme climax, Tammy yells with ultimate excitement, "Sweetssssssss!!!!!"

Once their climax is over they lay sweating and out of breath. "Ahhhhhhhhh!!!! Damn you were good!" she smiles. "Just like old times."

"Suga', I'm always good and don't you ever forget that shit! Hell, you can take my shit to the bank and lock it up in a safe deposit box it's so good!" Sweets seriously jokes.

"Yes you are, but this time you were better than I ever remembered!" Tammy kisses his neck, back, arms, and chest while he lays numb in the middle of the bed.

In an arrogant tone, Sweets smiles, "Yeah, I was, wasn't I!" Then he gets up to go to the shower.

"Where you going?" she tries pulling him back to her bed.

"I need to take a shower and get out of here. I got to pay some more bills."

Not Quite Good Enough

"You're leaving already? I thought we would go for another round."

"Another time baby, another time. I squeezed you in tonight. I have other clients I'm committed to see who have standing appointments, I can't keep them waiting too long." He gets into the shower with Tammy joining him.

Even though her most treasured desire felt pains of tenderness from all the rough and wild sex, once she was inside the shower with him, she ignored the pain and relived her yet again sexual yearning. As she caressed his soapy body next to hers, his manhood began to raise to great heights, when she placed him inside of her.

"Wait, I don't have a condom on." he warned.

"I don't care anymore, I just want to feel your power deep inside of me." She said while gently stroking him. As she held on tightly, she continued to fondle him with her love, allowing the hot streaming water to drizzle down her back.

Shortly after, she dropped to her knees, allowing her warm mouth to softly caress his well-endowed manhood with her love, causing him to moan out loud, "Ahhh, shit girl, that feels good. Damn, that feels good!" he says as he enjoys the pleasure.

After several minutes of another round of heated sex, each of them again reach their peaking climaxes. Once their desires are fully reached, Sweets had to cut things short and prepare to leave to handle his other business obligations.

"Ok now, that's enough." he gently pushes her away from his silky wet body. "Baby I gotta come back another time when I'm not in such a rush." He gently kisses her lips.

"Ahhh, just a little longer, please?" she begs while caressing his most intimate asset.

"Baby, as much as I want to stay longer, I gotta go. But call me, I promise I'll come back and stay longer." Quickly getting out of the shower he dresses and gets ready to leave.

T' La June

With her body still wet, Tammy jumps out the shower, puts on her bathrobe, and follows him to the door. "Ok, I'll let you go since you promised to come back." She slips him a wad of cash. "Here's a little sumthin, sumthin for your fast and personal house call. Especially since it's been so long, and WAS extra special for me. I also added a little more in there for you, just to show you just how much I appreciate you for squeezing me in. Remember, keep these meetings of ours, our little secret." She kisses him on his neck as he looks down at the cash and smiles.

"Yeah, I know you're a big time doctor now who can't be seen with an unprofessional brotha like me. That's alright, everybody's gotta do what they gotta do. Sweet daddy is just here to please, not to tease. So, as long as you're happy, I'm happy. Suga', my lips are sealed. Besides, it's all cool. I don't mind playing doctor myself every once in awhile by making house calls to you. Just call me Dr. Sweetness who makes you feel good. Next time I come, wear your doctor's uniform so I can really see you in action." Sweets smiles and kisses Tammy.

"I will. You were great tonight!"

"I aim to please Suga."

"Please you did! Believe me, I'm more than pleased. In fact, I'm going to have to use your number more often. I think I'm going to be needing a doctor more often Dr. Sweetness," she teases.

"Dr. Sweetness will be ready and waiting just for you. So call me anytime Dr. Jones! See ya suga'!" He gives Tammy one last passionate tongue kiss before he leaves. The kiss is so good Tammy holds him over for another one while squeezing his butt, then smiles and opens the door. Before letting him out the door she looks outside to make sure no one sees him and hurries him out. Tammy quietly closes the door and smiles. She is feeling totally satisfied, pleasurably raw, and exhausted, knowing tonight, she would have sweet dreams!

Not Quite Good Enough

Eleven - *One Night Stand*

It's seven in the evening and Mae May has just come home from work and is extremely tired. Her kids are crying, they're dirty, and chasing each other throughout the house. Her mother, Emma Jean, is sitting in front of a TV that's blasting loud. She is smoking a cigarette, drinking a beer, and watching a recorded version of the Oprah Winfrey show. Emma Jean is still dressed in her pajamas with rollers in her hair.

Mae May picks up her four and a half year old son. "What's wrong Bear? Why you hollerin' like that?" He continues crying. Upset, she yells at her mom and asks, "Momma, has he been crying like this all day long? His eyes are swollen."

Emma Jean, didn't know Mae May came home because the TV was so loud that she didn't hear her calling.

"Momma, I'm talking to you, has Bear been hollerin' like this all day?" Mae May repeats going over to the television set and turning it off.

"Hey, turn back on my TV. Oprah is getting ready to tell these young girls that they don't need to be sleeping around with so many different men because they're hoe's." Emma Jean looks directly at Mae May and says, "You need to hear this more than me."

Mae May brushes off the sarcasm and responds, "Yeah, yeah, yeah." She angrily asks, "So why is Bear crying so much?"

In a hateful tone, Emma Jean responds, "Ain't nothing wrong with that boy. His ass is just spoiled, that's all." Emma Jean gets up from the couch and gives Bear the bottle that was on the floor. "Here boy, take this bottle and shut the hell up. You're getting on my damn nerves. I can't even watch my show. Hush up before I give you something to cry about!" He spits out the sour tasting bottle and throws it to the floor. "Boy, I said take this damn bottle." Emma Jean

T' La June

demands and attempts to force it in his mouth.

    Mae May takes the bottle away. "Don't shove it down his throat, you'll choke him, damn you." Then she smells it, "Damnnn! Momma, this milk is sour, no wonder he doesn't want it. How long has it been out?" Mae May goes to the kitchen to get a fresh bottle and returns to the living room.

    Uninterested in the conversation, Emma Jean brushes Mae May off. "I don't know. I gave it to him this morning. Hell, I can't help it if he didn't drink it all when I gave it to him. Hell, he's a spoiled-ass brat, that's all." Emma Jean sits back down, turns on the television, takes a puff from her cigarette, and takes a sip of her beer. "Ahhh, this taste good," she says. She then holds the cold beer up toward her grandson and grins. Mae May shakes her head in disappointment and begins picking up toys left on the floor.

    Mae May's four year old daughter, Boo, who comes up to her sucking her thumb, says, "Momma where you been?" She reaches to be picked up.

    "Hey Boo, I been at work, how you doing baby girl?" Mae May picks up her daughter and places her in the other arm and kisses her cheek.

    Suddenly the two and three year old girls, Nay Nay & Tay Tay, notice that Mae May is home. They run to her, "Momma! Momma!" They also try to jump into her arms by pulling the other two down by their feet.

    Mae May puts down the older two kids and picks up the younger ones, "Ya'll's noses are nasty. Go get me some toilet tissue so I can clean your noses." Then she yells at her mom who is in the kitchen getting another beer out of the refrigerator, "Momma, why do they look so damn dirty?"

    "Cause I ain't had time to clean em', that's why. I had to pay close attention to my talk shows and soap operas because today

Not Quite Good Enough

is cliffhanger Friday. Now, I'm catching up with the Oprah episodes I had to tape this week because their bad asses kept hollerin' and begging for something to eat."

Mae May's tone becomes more annoyed. "Momma, I can't be coming home to all this damn noise. I've been working hard all day long. I shouldn't have to hear all this noise every time I come in the door." She picks up her youngest kids, while signaling the older ones to follow her to the kitchen. "Come on ya'll, let Momma get you something to eat so you can go to bed. All this damn noise is getting on my goddamn nerves." Mae May fumes as she rattles through the cabinets to find the kids something simple and quick to eat.

Upset with her daughter's comments, Emma Jean fires back loud so Mae May can hear her, "Mae May, your kids have been getting on my damn nerves all day long with their spoiled little asses. So, don't come in here with all that bullshit!" She rants as she focuses her attention back on the television.

After eating, the kids go to their beds to watch a DVD cartoon. After they fall asleep, Mae May goes through the house picking up the rest of the mess they've left behind. When she comes back into the living room, her mother has fallen asleep on the couch with the television still on. She is snoring while holding onto an empty 40 ounce bottle of beer. Soon after, Mae May sneaks out the house to go to a club.

Once in the club, loud music is playing. The room is very dark and filled with party goers. Mae May walks in and searches for Marque', who she finds sitting at a table with a male friend. "Hey Ya'll, what's up? How's the party tonight?" She says with excitement, ready to dance.

"It's cool!" Marque' said. He then introduces her to his friend for the evening. "Mae May, this is Tommy." Tommy extends his hand to shake hers and smiles.

"Hello." Tommy says as Mae May extends her hand in return.
"Hi Tommy, nice to meet you."

With a cocky attitude, Marque' says to Mae May, "Girl, what took you so long? We've been here for over an hour waiting for your black ass."

Mae May looks at Marque' with a look on her face indicating, 'Oh no you didn't just say that to me,' and says, "Excuse me for being late, but I had to feed and put my bad ass kids to bed. Momma was into her TV shows and getting her drink on. I had to make sure everyone was asleep before I could leave. I sure didn't want to give Momma another thing to talk smack about if she knew I was going out again to party."

Marque' laughs, "See, even you have to admit your kids are bad."

"How many kids you got?" Tommy asks.

"Four"

"How old are they?" Tommy continues.

"Four - almost five, four and a half, three, and two."

He laughs, "Damn girl, you've been busy."

Marque' jokingly agrees, "Ummm hummm."

Mae May proudly displays a cocky and confident attitude. "Heyyyyyy, what can I say!" She looks around the room and carries on. "So where's the waitress? Because after a long day at work, and going home to a house that looked and sounded like a tornado hit it, I need a damn drink!" Suddenly a song Mae May likes came out the speakers, causing her to become excited. "Heyyyyyy, that's my song. Where's a man that I can dance with? Cause I'm ready to get my party onnnnn!" Mae May begins dancing in her seat and snapping her fingers to the music. Marque' and Tommy totally ignore Mae May and engage in a passionate kiss, causing Mae May to become jealous.

"Hell, if it's gonna be like that I'm gonna find me somebody to suck on, see ya!"

Not Quite Good Enough

Mae May gets up and walks around the room; finds a man to dance with, and then dances very seductively. The mystery dancer is enjoying every moment of her lustful dance. He's smiling like there's no tomorrow, while starring at her body. He begins to erotically lick his lips in an attempt to sexually lure Mae May. The type of alluring gesture made famous by L.L. Cool J.. Soon after, she boldly samples a taste and said, "Ummm, you have some juicy lips. They taste like honey." She flirts.

"I got something else that tastes a lot like honey too, you wanna try it out and see?" He flirts back.

With a lustful look in her eyes, Mae May answers seductively, "Yeah, my car or yours?"

He whispers deep in her ear, causing her ear to sweat from the emotion, "Mine." He takes her hand and they quickly go outside.

Shortly after, she finds herself in the backseat of his car. He locks the door and immediately, they begin stripping off each other's clothes. While she's sitting up straight, he starts going south on her as she enjoys the journey. Later, he comes up for air and begins to slide her totally down on the seat.ABruptly, Mae May stops him as he attempts to get on top of her. "Wait." She said.
"What happened?" He looks around.

"Let me get on top of you." Mae May pats her hair to make sure it's still in place and continues, "I just got my hair done and I ain't about to mess it up for nobody!" Surprised by the request, he rolls her over to reverse the position so he's on the bottom and the sex begins.

While they're in the moment of pleasure, Mae May's voluptuous 42 double D breast are bouncing in his face. He cheerfully opens his mouth wide and samples the taste they bring. They proceed with having sex.

"Ummmm, ahhhhh!" Were the sounds heard coming from his car as he enjoyed the pleasure of the moment.

A few short minutes later, Mae May began looking at her long fingernails, making sure they hadn't broke. She was waiting for him to insert his penis inside her vagina so she could enjoy the pleasure. She thought, "Is he inside of me yet? I sure can't feel a goddamn thing. With all this humping and groaning he's doing, I sure hope he gets his dick inside of me before I dry up." She continues stroking him, hoping she can help guide his penis inside her awaiting vagina. "Ohhh, ahhhh! You feel sooo good." Mae May says, as she fakes the sounds of lovemaking pleasure in order to make him feel good.

Shortly after, he lets out a loud sigh of relief, and stops his stoking movement because the sex is over. He comes up from underneath her body smiling, and says, "Damn girl, you were good!"

Knowing she hadn't been satisfied yet, Mae May is surprised by his comment and performance. She moves over from him, looks down at his deflated penis, and thinks, "It's over already? Damn! Not another one of these assholes who can't screw. Why do I keep getting these fools who can't screw worth a fuck? Why do I keep wasting my damn time?"

Feeling proud of his accomplishment, he's beaming with satisfaction while putting on his clothes and says, "Girl, I'm a have to hit this coochie again. What's your name, and give me your number!"

Mae May frowns at his suggestion and begins putting back on her clothes. With a sarcastic tone she blasts him, "I don't give out my name or telephone number to just anybody."
Surprised by her answer, he questions her. "Well damn, why not?"
"You're a stranger." she says.

He looks at her with a disappointed look and said, "Now ain't that some shit. Hell, you didn't seem to think I was a stranger when I was eating your pussy."
Mae May ignores him and continues getting dressed.

Upset with her reaction he responds, "Oh, so I see how it is,

Not Quite Good Enough

this was just a hit and run for you!"

"Yeah, that's exactly what it was, a damn hit and run. Except the hit was too quick for me so I gotta run. First of all, it wasn't long enough for me to even be pleased. Also, when you ate my pussy you kept biting me with your damn teeth, which hurt like hell. All that damn hollerin' and heavy breathing you were doing in my ear didn't do a damn thing for me. Instead, it made my ear sweat from your bad breath. So I don't think I'll be having sex with you evah again. In fact, you wasted my damn time. So I'm outta of here." Mae May slams the car door and strolls back toward the club.

He sticks his head out the door and says, "Damn baby come back, please! I was just warming up. I promise, it'll be better the next time around. Please!" He pleads out loud as she keeps walking. Other's in the parking lot are looking and laughing as she keeps walking, giving him her 'fuck you' finger.

Then she stops and turns around, "You only get one time to prove yourself with me and you failed. So there won't be another time." She opens the door and goes back inside the club. She then finds herself sitting at an empty table, smoking a cigarette, and waiting for her next quest.

T' La June

Twelve - *The Make-Over*

Sophia, dressed in grey overalls, is at work at the recycling warehouse. Aaron, her co-worker says with a compliment, "WOW you look GREAT!"

Sophia begins blushing, continuing to put away a load of cans, "Thank you."

Shortly after, another co-worker Brad is surprised by what he sees in Sophia. He begins smiling from ear to ear. "Wow, look at you. You look beautiful. Looks like somebody has a date tonight."

"Yeah, that's what I was thinking." Aaron agrees. "Must be somebody real special. I've never seen your hair and makeup look so nice. You look great Sophia! So, who's the lucky guy?" He teases.

The once plain-Jane girl now looks like a beautifully crafted camera ready fashion model.

Sophia blown away by the compliments continues blushing. "Thanks for the compliments. Sorry, there's no lucky guy unless one of you losers is taking me out and treating," she jokes. "Otherwise, the only place I'm going tonight is to bed, alone."

"Why don't we do the usual and go to the pub down the street. Since you look so nice, I'll treat you for a drink." offers Brad. "You can't go through all the trouble of looking so nice and not go somewhere to show yourself off, besides work."

Aaron seconds the comment and adds, "That sounds good, I'll join you guys."

Sophia becomes disappointed by the conversation. "The pub? You mean I paid all this money to get my hair and makeup done, to look nice, and that's the only place I'm good enough to go to? Damn, you just made me feel real good, never mind." She huffs and goes back to work.

Aaron shakes his head, smiles and takes a step back. He

Not Quite Good Enough

says, "Brad, you're in trouble now buddy."

Brad then feels bad and tries to make things right. "Nooo! Sophia, I didn't mean it like that, I'm sorry."

Sophia turns away from him and piles another load of cans in a container. With a sad expression, she then says, "well, that's what it sounded like to me."

Aaron is confused by her comment and sad attitude and asks, "What's the matter? He said he wants to take you out and treat you to a drink, isn't that good enough?"

Upset with his tone and question, Sophia fires back at Aaron, "No, it's not good enough. After all this work, I'm worth more than a cheap drink at the local pub. Besides, the pub is not going out."

Brad is puzzled, "What's up with the pub? We always go there to chill."

Disappointed, Sophia, pats her hair and bats her newly installed eyelashes as she responds, "This is not the pub look. So, never mind. I'll just go home."

Aaron's cell phone rings, he smiles and responds, "Ahhh, saved by the bell! This conversation is getting too dangerous for me. Brad, you handle this situation on your own. I'm out of here."

Alone now, Brad takes Sophia's hand and passionately looks into her eyes. He then speaks with great compassion, "Ok, let's start over." She smiles as he continues. "Sophia, you look very nice today. Would you like to go out to dinner with me tonight?"

Surprised by his kindness, she blushes and says, "Sure, but only if you're serious."

"I'm as serious as a heart attack." Then he softly kisses her on her cheek.

She really blushes, "Ok, what time should we meet? And is this a real date, or a, just two friends going out to get a bite to eat date with no strings attached?"

T' La June

"Let's just call it a fun night kinda date with two good friends."

She becomes disappointed and continues to work. Sophia then says, "Never mind, I'll just eat at home, alone. At least that way I can look into the mirror and give myself compliments without feeling humiliated." Angry, she starts walking away and goes back to work. Puzzled, Brad grabs her hand and pulls her back, "What did I say now?" he says.

Sophia sighs heavily, "I don't want to go out with someone just for fun anymore. I'm tired of always feeling like I'm one of the guys. I want someone to wine and dine me, and treat me like a real lady. That's why I went to all the trouble of getting a new look. Is that too much to ask for?"

Brad brings Sophia closer to him and whispers in her ear, "I don't know if you know, but I've always had my eye on you. I just thought you were taken or not interested. I thought you enjoyed just hanging out as friends."

Surprised and blushing like a school girl in love, Sophia answers, "Who me not interested? Hell, I didn't know you were interested in me." She bats her eyelashes whole glowing with happiness.

Brad continues his whisper. "Ok, let's call it a real date. Let's start with tonight and see what happens later. Let's also keep it to ourselves so we don't get in trouble with the boss or start any rumors around the warehouse."

Sophia is unsure with his offer and pleasantly smiles, "Are you sure? I don't want you going out with me because you feel sorry for me."

"Feel sorry for you? Oh nooooo, I don't feel sorry for you. That's not what I feel at all. Sophia, you're a nice lady. Like I said, I've always admired you and thought you were cool. I just never told you. I wouldn't have asked you to go out if I wasn't serious. So, what do you say, tonight at seven?" He has a sad, but funny, puppy dog grin

Not Quite Good Enough

on his face.

Excited, she quickly answers, "Sure, where should we meet?"

"How about I pick you up at your house?"

"Ok, I'll see you at seven." She beams with joy and attempts to go back to work until Brad is out of her sight. Once he's out of her sight, she pulls out her cell phone and send a text message to her best friend Vicki, "Girlll, I've got something to tell you when I get home. I'm sooo excited! :)" She quickly presses send, closes her phone, and gets back to work seconds before her supervisor walks by.

SEVERAL HOURS LATER

Sophia arrives home from work and calls Vicki, "Hello?" Vicki says. "Hey Vicki, it's me Sophia, what's going on?"

"Hey girl, I just got home from work and I'm lying down because I'm tired. I'm getting ready to eat and then go to bed. What you up too? And what's so exciting that you have to tell me?"

Sophia is so excited she can hardly contain her emotions, "Girl, I got a date. I'm going out tonight with Brad."

Vicki is surprised and confused; "Who the hell is Brad?"

"A guy I work with at the warehouse. He's coming to pick me up at seven to take me out to dinner."

Vicki tries to act uninterested; "Umm, good for you. Maybe now you can get some dick like you've been wanting and quit trippin'."

Smiling, "My thoughts exactly, because it's been awhile since I've had some real dick. Hell, it's been so long I've almost forgotten what a real one feels like." she laughs. "The dildos are great when you're desperate, but now they're getting real boring. I want some real skin inside of my dry coochie and a warm man to hold in my arms." Sophia fantasies.

"So how did all this date mess happen?"

Sophia is more than ready to tell the entire story. "Remember,

I told you I was going to get my hair done last night?"

"Yeah, what about it?"

"Well, when I went to work I got a few compliments and then Brad asked me out."

"So you're telling me that all it took was for you to get a new hairdo to get a date?"

"Yes, that's exactly what I'm telling you, in addition to the extra make-over treatments I added."

Vicki is jealous but acts interested. "Good for you. I hope you have fun."

"Damn girl, do you think you could be a little more excited for me? Because you sure didn't say that like you meant it."

"I'm not sure if I did. From the way I see things, he'll get his way and then your feelings will be hurt, just like all the other times. I don't know why you waste your time with these crazy men anyway. I'm done with em'."

Upset with her answer, Sophia blasts back, "It would be nice if you could try to be a little positive for once in your damn life! That's why you don't have a man, you're too damn negative. So, if you can't wish me well, then don't say anything. As a matter of fact, I just won't tell you about my date or any others from now on."

Vicki tries to play things off like she cares, "Damn girl, quit trippin'. Forget what I said and have fun. I'm just tired, that's all. Call me when you get home."

Sophia wasn't going to allow Vicki's comments to upset her so she ends the conversation. "Ok, I gotta get dressed. He'll be here in an hour. Talk to you later."

Vicki could tell Sophia was upset and wanted to clear the air. "Wait, before you go. Really, have fun and call me when you get home, or better yet, call me after you get some dick and tell me all about your experience. At least one of us will have some warm arms

Not Quite Good Enough

wrapped around us tonight."

Sophia smiles at the suggestion, "Ok girl, I will." She rushes off the phone. "Talk to you later. I gotta go."

"Ok you crazy girl, bye." Vicki says while grinning.

"Hey, maybe I can stop by your house real quick tomorrow morning before I go to work, so you can see the new look Marque' created for me." Sophia says.

"Sure, that'll be good. See you then, bye."

"Ok, see you tomorrow, bye." Sophia hangs up the phone and prepares for her date. In the meantime, Vicki goes to a mirror and rearranges her hairstyle. She wonders if a make-over would help her.

SEVERAL HOURS LATER...

Tammy and Cindy are eating at a five star restaurant when Sophia and Brad arrive. Cindy is surprised by their arrival and points out Sophia to Tammy. "That's the lady I met at the beauty shop last night." Cindy says.

Tammy frowns, with a surprised and stuck-up look she responds, "Who her?"

"Yes her."

Tammy begins judging, "You mean to tell me that Marque' did her hair? She doesn't look like she can afford him."

Cindy smiles, approving the new look. "Yes, and he did her makeup too. Girl, you should have seen her before he did his magic. She was a hot mess to say the least." Cindy makes frowning motions, gagging, and laughing to express herself and continues. "She was tore up from the floor up. Believe me when I say that she looks ten times better today than she looked before he finished with her. That's probably why she's on a date. Marque' hooked her up! She was just complaining about not being able to get a date. Look at her now. Sista girl got it going on now." Cindy smiles with happiness.

Tammy acts uninterested. "What ever! And quit talking like such a ghetto girl. Somebody might hear you."
Cindy looks at Tammy and smiles, "Sounds like you're jealous!"

Tammy rolls her eyes and with a sarcastic tone responds, "Who me, jealous of homey looking girl over there? If you ask me, she still looks like a hot mess. Hell, my looks and status run circles around her. So why should I be jealous of her?"

"Because she's with a man and your not!" Cindy teases, "Hater! You just need to get you some dick."

Tammy smiles and begins thinking about her night with Sweets. Cindy continues talking, "I guess it has been a long time for both of us."
Tammy beams with delight and whispers, "Speak for yourself."
"Did you say something?" Cindy asks.

Tammy quickly regains her composure and responds, "No. I didn't say a thing. That was just my stomach growling. Where's our waiter?" She looks around the room to fake-out Cindy. Then she smiles as she again reminisces about last night with Sweets.

Cindy looks at Tammy with a surprised look and said, "Why do you have that silly grin on your face? What are you thinking about?"

Tammy quickly changes her thought. "I'm not grinning. I was just thinking about how that lady must have looked before Marque' worked on her. Damnnnn, the thought haunts me!!!"

"Yeah, it was pretty scary!" They continue to eat salsa and chips, drink wine, and finish their conversation.

"We were so busy at work today. You never told me what you did last night." Cindy asks while Tammy works hard to tune into her conversation to avoid from daydreaming. "I tried calling you after I left the shop, but your phone went straight to voice mail."

Tammy immediately chokes on her chips as she thinks of an answer. "Girl, I was so tired that I went right to bed when I got home.

Not Quite Good Enough

I unplugged my phone so I didn't hear it ring."

Cindy accepts her excuse and gets excited about sharing her story. "Girllllll, let me tell you what happened in the beauty shop last night." She shakes her head and smiles. "For one, Marque' and Mae May are wayyyy crazy. They had us laughing all night long. Those two are so funny they should have a comedy show." Tammy is listening, while thinking more about Sweets as Cindy continues with her story. "Then Mae May told us the story about some guy named Sweets who's known around town as a good screw, otherwise a gigolo hoe." Cindy said.

Tammy suddenly spits out the wine, causing it to fly across the table.

"Are you alright?"

Embarrassed, Tammy covers up her true feelings, "Yes, I'm fine. It was just funny what you said." She grabs her napkin and cleans up her mess.

After knowing Tammy is alright Cindy continues; "Girl, the way they were talking about Sweets, and as horny as I am for a man, hell I was ready to find him and get me a good ass screw."

"Girl please, don't lower your standards on a man like him. But yeah, I heard all about this so called Sweets. I would never settle for someone like him. The man doesn't even have a real job." Tammy wipes her mouth, throws back her hair weave and continues acting prim and proper.

"Well, from what they were saying, brotha man doesn't need a real job. He seems to have plenty of women taking care of him.

They say he's living rather well from the support of those who enjoy and can afford, his company." she winks.

Tammy is getting upset with Cindy's comments. "Is that all you ever think about is getting laid? Damn girl, there are more things in life besides getting laid. Let's change the subject. I'm tired of hearing about people screwing. Besides, why do they keep bringing him up anyway?"

Cindy is surprised by Tammy's behavior but answers. "He came into the shop before I left and the talk was on. Girlll, that man is fine!! I can see why they keep bringing him up. He came to get his nails done, said they were dull and cracking. Then he started telling us about some hoochy's house he had just left and got paid big time. Hell, as good as he looks, I'll be his hoochy anytime! I got a few bucks to spare, heyyyyy!" Cindy laughs as she begins dancing in her seat. Tammy suddenly chokes again as tears fall down her cheeks.

"What's wrong girl? Are you sick or something? Do you need some water or fresh air?"

Tammy can barely speak, but answers, "No thank you, I'm fine. I just keep getting something caught in my throat. What exactly did this guy Sweets say?"

"I thought you weren't interested."

Tammy becomes fidgety as she waits for the answers. "Just tell me what he said. He was probably lying like he always does."

"And how would you know if he was lying or not?"

"He used to date one of my friends. Just tell me what he said."

Cindy looks at Tammy with a weird look and continues. "He said he had just laid some lady who thinks she's all that. He said that she wanted him so bad that she didn't want him to leave. He said he tore up her coochie and made her scream his name over and over again. Girl, he just kept going on and on about how he made this lady want him more. He was soooo funny that we were all cracking up while listening to him."

Tammy suddenly becomes embarrassed. "What else did he say?"

Cindy is really shocked by Tammy's interest and questions her, "Boy, you sure are interested in hearing about someone you think is beneath you, aren't you?"

Not Quite Good Enough

Tammy becomes upset and softly explodes to defend herself, "Just tell me what he said and quit tripping. I told you my friend used to date him. He may have been talking about her and I need to know so I can tell her. I hope she finally gets over him and drops him. That's all, so go on."

With a surprised look on her face and an uncomfortable feeling, Cindy answers. "He didn't say too much more, other than a guy's normal brag! Again, why are YOU so interested in what Sweets said?"

Knowing Cindy had suspicions, Tammy rose up and in a bold tone protects her interest and said. "Like I said, I'm not interested for me, but for my friend. You know I couldn't be seen with a man who ain't got a job. So I'm definitely not asking for me. Besides, I'm going to see Chad. Remember him? He is the sweet rich guy who loves me to death and can't get enough of me! I was just asking about Sweets because I heard so many stories about him from my friend. She has always said that Sweets is known for telling a lot of lies, that's all. Nothing more! So can we drop the subject please."

"Ok, if you say so." Cindy goes along with Tammy's story and chances the conversation. "Isn't Chad the white businessman you dated before?"

Tammy took the opportunity to act excited and ditch any suspicions Cindy had. "Yes, he called me last night and said he would also call tonight. So, are you done yet because I'm ready to go home in case he calls?"

"Almost, hold on. Oh yeah, here's your invitation to the big Valentine's Day party."

Tammy looks at the invitation. "So, I see that Marque's shop is having another one." Then she goes into deep thought. "I hope Sweets doesn't come to this one. I would not be comfortable in the same room with him and other people around us."

Cindy is puzzled by Tammy's uneasy reaction, but quickly finishes eating. "Ok, I'm ready now." They get up and leave. Cindy waves at Sophia as she passes her on her way out the door. Sophia smiles and waves back; then focuses her attention back on Brad. Brad is smiling and looking deep into Sophia's eyes. "Wow, I'm really enjoying myself."

"Me too." Sophia says.

Brad takes Sophia's hand and looks deeper into her eyes. "Sophia you look beautiful tonight. I haven't seen you look this beautiful since I've known you. Whatever you did to yourself I love t! Keep up this new look."

Sophia blushes, "I guess I will if I can hold your undivided attention like this." She fantasizes about having sex with him when she gets home. She feels she finally found her dick that she's been searching for. With his muscular brown and rugged body, that stands over six feet high, Brad isn't too bad to look at himself.

"I always knew you were nice, but I never took the time to really get to know you. I'd like to take you out again, if that's alright." Sophia blushes. "Sure, that sounds good to me."

The music playing in the room is soft and slow. "May I have this dance?" Brad asks as he reaches for her hand.

Sophia is surprised by the offer. "Sure! I'd love to." Brad gets up, takes her hand as they walk to the dance floor and slow dance. He's holding her ever so close and lays her head on his shoulders while she melts into his arms.

All of a sudden Sophia steps on Brad's feet and trips. They laugh. "I'm sorry. I haven't danced in so long I've forgotten how to follow a man's lead."

"That's ok. We'll dance a little longer so you can get the hang of it." Holding her closer, he kisses her cheek. Sophia smiles, feeling like the luckiest lady in the world.

Not Quite Good Enough

As the night goes on, they enjoy each other's company. They are learning things about each other they never knew.

A few hours later they arrive back at Sophia's house. Brad walks her to her front door and kisses her on the cheek and she blushes.

"Ahhh, that was cute."

"Cute is all I get?" Brads asks.

"Cute is all you gave."

"Well, how's this?" He leans over, hugs Sophia and gives her a juicy tongue kiss that seemed to last a lifetime. Then he comes up for air, releasing fireworks in their minds.

Sophia smiles, "Now that's more like it! Would you like to come in?" She was hoping for a yes answer.

Brad respectfully smiles. "I sure would, but I don't think I should. I think we should take things slow for now."

Sophia is disappointed with his answer. "Is this your way of letting me down easy?"

"Not at all. Like I said earlier, I do want to get to know you better. I've always admired you and thought you were a great person. So now that we've taken the first step of an official date, I really don't want to rush anything. Do you understand?"

Sophia is upset with Brad's request and feels rejected. "Yeah, I understand. This is the last time we'll go out on a date, right? Admit it, it's cool, I can handle it."

"No, no you have it all wrong, I truly enjoyed your company. I just want to respect you and take things slow, that's all. We need to get to know each other better before jumping into anything too quickly.

After tonight, being with you like this, I see a whole new Sophia. I would rather get to know you for the long haul." She blushes as he continues. "So what about dinner Friday night?"

Shocked by his request Sophia questions him, "This Friday night?"

"Yes, if that's alright with you."

She is extremely happy and answers, "Ok then, sure. I'd like that." She blushes again. "So, I guess I'll see you in three days."

"Yes you will, but don't forget I'll see you tomorrow at work, that is if you don't call in sick." they laugh.

"No, I won't. I'll be there bright and early."

"Good, but remember, this has to be our little secret at work so we don't get fired." he reminds her.

Smiling, Sophia said, "My lips are sealed."

"Good, but may I have the pleasure of unsealing them one last time before I go home?"

"Sure." Brad passionately kisses Sophia one last time. Another kiss that seems to last forever. He then gets into his car, and leaves with both of them feeling happy.

Not Quite Good Enough

Thirteen - *The Hook Up*

"Damn I have a hangover." Marque' said. He does his best to get in the groove of working after a long night of partying.

Mae May is also moving slow. "Me too. So don't talk too loud. In fact, turn down the CD player. I'm getting a headache from all that drinking last night."

"Girl, what happened to you? You disappeared on us." said Marque'

In a nonchalant tone, Mae May answers, "I got my party on and hooked up with this guy. Then I hooked up with another one and went home."

"Are you telling me that you got laid twice last night?"

Mae May began smiling. "No, I'm not telling you that, but that's what I did. The first one wasn't that good, but the second one made up for the first one. In fact, he really made up. He was damn good and lasted for a long time! Hell, my pussy is still throbbing from all the sex I had with him. I'm lovin' every bit of the pain. Makes me remember the night much better," she brags.

Marque' laughs, "Damnnnnnn girl, you screwed two guys in one night? You nasty hoe!" he teases.

"Don't act surprised bitch because it ain't the first time. Look who's calling the kettle black, you freaky hoe. How many did you screw last night?"

Marque' smiles while attempting to brush off the conversation, "Yeah, yeah, yeah! You're just hatin'! My business is my business."

"Hell, I got my advice from you. Ain't that how you do it? Since when has your business been YOUR business? You tell every goddamn thing that goes on with you, so don't stop now." she teases back.

Bragging, Marque' reveals his business with pride. "Welllll, if you must know, I also got laid last night. First from Tommy, the guy I was sitting next too at the table that I introduced you too. Then I went home to my sweety. He hooked me up with some more before I went to sleep. So I'm feeling pretty damn happy today myself," he massages his behind as he smiles.

"See, so who you calling a hoe, hoe!" Mae May laughs along with their customers, who are totally into their conversation.

Bragging again, Marque' goes farther into detail. "Mannnn, the one I had last night was off the chain! He worked me good. I learned a few new moves from him that I couldn't wait to show my sweety when I got home."

"Where did you guys hook up? Did you leave the club?"

"No stayed right there and did our thang in one of the restroom stalls, where I always go for a quicky." Marque' leans against the wall in a spread eagle position to demonstrate. He moans with his eyes closed, and then smiles.

"You bitch." Mae May laughs, then throws a filing board at him as he ducks and grins as she continues. "Which one was it, the men's or women's?" she teases.

"Men's, you bitch!" he laughs.

"You Freakin' hoe!" she clowns around.

"Remember it takes one to know one, hoe!" Marque' teases back and says, "My question to you is do you feel as good as I do this morning?" He looks at her with a puzzled look on his face, waiting for her answer.

"Hellll yeahhh and probably better!" Mae May smiles as she dances in her chair.

"Bitch, I don't think that can ever happen." Marque' said as he finishes his customer's hair.

Vicki walks in to the shop and greets everyone. Marque' says. "Hey Vicki, what brings you in?"

Not Quite Good Enough

"Hey Marque'. I have a few hours to spare and was hoping you could fit me in today?" Without saying a word, Marque' gives her a crazy look. She continues, "The look you gave Sophia was very nice. It was so nice that she got a date. I figured that maybe you could work some of your magic on me so that I can also get someone special." She looks at Marque' with puppy dog eyes, pleading for his help.

Marque' puts his hand on his hip and scolds her. "Now listen here bitch, you know I don't take walk-in's." She looks really sad, sticking out her lip. He smiles and continues, "Damn girl, wipe away that pathetic puppy dog look, I'm just joking with you." She smiles and he continues. "However, since you know I'm cool like that, and you're a long time customer, I'll take your ass since my next appointment canceled. So if you can wait for about twenty minutes I'll start on you next."

Vicki is happy with his answer and responds, "That'll work." She sits down and reads a magazine while she waits.

T' La June

Fourteen - *Mystery Caller*

It's mid-morning Tuesday, Tammy is in the examining room with a patient while Cindy sits at the front desk, the phone rings. "Doctor's office, may I help you?"
A pleasant male voice inquires, "Yes, may I speak to the doctor please?"

Cindy is amused by the mysterious voice and answers, "I'm sorry, the doctor can't come to the phone right now. She's busy with her patients. May I help you?"

"No thank you. I would like to speak directly to the doctor. I'm a personal friend of hers. I want to surprise her. Can you please ask her to come to the phone for just one quick minute?" Cindy smiles at the request.

She catches Tammy in the hallway before she goes to examine another patient and whispers, "Tammy," she gestures her to hurry, "Come here. Some guy is on the phone asking for you. He said he's a personal friend of yours. He sounds real sexy. Ummm, holding out on me I see?" Cindy smiles, and watches Tammy go toward the phone.

Tammy is surprised by the request. She picks up the phone and walks around the corner so she could have a private conversation. With curiosity she answers, "Hello? This is Dr. Jones. Who's this?"

The sexy male voice responds, "Hello Dr. this is a good friend. Do you recognize my voice?"

Tammy is not amused. She replies whispering in a nasty, sarcastic tone, "No I don't, so stop wasting my time. I have patients waiting for me. So either you're going to tell me who this is or I'm hanging up the phone." Cindy eavesdropping from around the corner is puzzled by Tammy's tone and conversation. She remains quiet as she listens more.

"Damn, don't sound so mean. You didn't have a problem

Not Quite Good Enough

remembering who I was the other night when I arrested you and then we made love. This is Sweet Daddy with plenty of lovin' for you Suga'." Suddenly Tammy begins coughing. Cindy quickly appears from around the corner and pats her back. Tammy gives her the signal that she's alright and then shoo's her away. Cindy continues hiding so she can eavesdrop. Soon after a patient comes out the room and gets Cindy's attention. Cindy walks away disappointed that she can't continue eavesdropping.

Surprised by the caller, Tammy unpleasantly whispers. "How did you get this number? Why are you calling me at work?"

"I missed you and had a little time to spare this afternoon. Wanna get together?" Sweets asks in a cocky, confident tone.

Still whispering, Tammy gives him a piece of her mind. "Hell no! I don't want to spend any more time with you. I heard you went to Marque's shop, after you left my condo, and told everyone about us having sex. You even said that I paid you. I couldn't believe you told everyone how we had sex. You said everything you could think of and that isn't cool. So get lost and don't ever call or visit me again!" Tammy slams down the telephone, marches in to see a patient, and slams the door behind her.

Cindy sees Tammy's angered reaction and wonders, "Damn, who was that? I missed what she said, dammit!" she stumps her feet and continues, "Oh well, whoever it was sure did piss her off." Then she goes back to work feeling disappointed that she couldn't hear the entire conversation.

Shortly after, Tammy comes out of the patient's room and Cindy approaches her. "Damn girl, who was that on the phone? Because he sure pissed you off! Are you holding out on me or what? What's up?"

Tammy snaps, "Nothing's wrong. It was nothing. Just go back to work." She quickly walks away to attend to another patient, as Cindy looks puzzled.

Cindy's mind goes into overdrive as Tammy slams yet another door and thinks, "Ummm, this sounds like it may be something good. Let me check to see if the phone number shows up on caller ID. Maybe I can get to bottom of this bad attitude." Cindy goes back to the telephone to check out the caller ID and becomes disappointed again. "Damn, an unlisted number." She wonders, "Who was that? And what's going on?" She sits at her desk curious, then gets back to work.

Not Quite Good Enough

Fifteen - *Wanna Play House?*

"Thank you for taking me on such short notice." Vicki said to Marque'. She sits in his chair to get her hair and makeup done.

"Girlfriend, only because we go way back will I do this for you today. Consider this your lucky day and don't try to pull this shit anymore! You know I don't take walk-in's." Marque' scolds as he combs through Vicki's hair.

Happy to be in his chair, Vicki makes other conversation to change Marque's mood. "Marque' you hooked up Sophia's hair and makeup great yesterday. I was hoping you could do the same for me. Hell, the work you put into her even got her a date, and that bitch hasn't had a date in years. So, helpppppp!" She jokes.

With a joking look Marque' said, "For one, Sophia had an appointment." He reminds her as he pulls her head back while holding a handful of her hair, and looks into her eyes with a cynical look and continues, "Also because I know what the hell I'm doing. Therefore, I would say getting a date ain't hard once you've been in my chair. Even though with Sophia, that job did not come easy. She was here for a long damn time. I worked on that girl for so long that my fingers were hurting when I finished. Thank God she was my last client." he jokes. Marque's tone changes to serious. "Anyway, girllll Sophia told me some nasty shit about you."

Vicki surprised, looks at Marque' through the mirror. With an evil look on her face, ready to fight back, she said, "What did she say?"

"She said you're an evil bitch, and she can't stand your black ass!" Marque' keeps a straight and serious look on his face while waitting for Vicki's response.

Vicki turns completely around and looks at Marque'. She is shocked and ready for war. "The bitch said what? Oh hell no! I'mma kick her ass. What else did she say?"

Marque' falls out laughing, "Got ya bitch! She didn't say anything. I was just pulling your leg because your ass didn't make an appointment. Now I feel better."

Vicki is relieved. "Don't play with me like that. I was ready to get all up in her ass."

Marque' begins whispering. "And I'm sure you would. Or have you already? If you catch my drift."

"What's that suppose to mean?" Vicki is stunned by the comment.

"It can mean anything you want it to mean. You tell me. And don't forget I already know you want Sophia real bad, so don't lie. Don't you?"

"What do you mean, I want her real bad? She's my friend and that's it!"

"Vicki come on, don't pull that innocent shit with me. I know you girl. I know how you operate. Now, it might be another story for Sophia, but I know it's not for you. Bitch, I know you're working overtime on homegirl to give you a chance to play house with her. Now tell me it isn't true? Come on, look dead in my eyes and tell me it isn't true, because I know you, and I know the truth."

Vicki is surprised and amused by his accusations. "Where in the hell do you get your information from? Because you sure in hell don't know what you're talking about.

"Ummm hmmmm. Don't forget you've told me a few interesting stories in the past. Girl I know you play house, just like I do. And believe me, I play very well. I also know who wants to play." Marque' winks at Vicki and smiles.

Vicki acts upset but doesn't make a scene. "Marque' I haven't told you shit. You're just making up shit like you always do. Just do my hair and keep the smart ass comments to yourself."

"Ok, ok! I can see I ruffled your feathers, didn't I?" Vicki

Not Quite Good Enough

looks at him with an angered look but Marque' doesn't give in. "That's alright. It can be our little secret. I guess you're still not sure what side of the fence you want to play on. You still have time. Sophia isn't taken yet. But don't wait too long. She said she's gonna start getting her hair done every week so she can catch a man. And from what you've told me, it's already working. Hell, she may be married before long at the rate she's working it. So I wouldn't take too long honey." Marque' goes back to finishing Vicki's hair while she doesn't say a word.

T' La June

Sixteen - *Five Minute Sex*

It's late in the evening. Tammy has just arrived home from work. She begins taking off her clothes when the phone rings. She's so tired she doesn't answer and lets the answering machine do its job. "Hello, I can't come to the phone right now, please leave a message and I'll return your call as soon as I can, beeppppp." The caller begins talking; "Hey Tammy, it's me Cindy. You left work before we could talk. I'm worried about you. I hope everything is ok. Call me anytime. I'll be home."

Tammy shakes her head and smiles. "I knew Cindy would be calling to see who I was talking to at work. She's sooo nosey. But that information is staying with me."

Hungry and tired, with a growling stomach, Tammy opens the refrigerator thinking how nice it will be to bite into a piece of strawberry cheesecake. She looks inside her refrigerator when the phone rings. Again she lets the answering machine do its job. "Hello, I can't come to the phone right now, please leave a message and I'll return your call as soon as I can, beepppppp." She listens in. "Tammy, this is Chad. I was in the neighborhood and wanted to stop by if you were home." Tammy hurries to catch the phone and begins blushing. "Hi Chad!"

Chad is happy to hear her live voice said, "Hey Tammy. So you are home."

"Yes, I'm here. I was just screening my calls. I had a long day at work. I didn't want to talk to just anyone. But I'll talk to you." She's blushing.

"Well, if you're up for company, I'll stop by. I'm right around the corner."

"Sure, I'd love your company."

"You do still live in the same place, don't you? It has been

Not Quite Good Enough

awhile since I was at your house."

"Yes, I'm still here."

"Ok, I'll see you in ten minutes. I'll get us some wine. Is there anything else you need for me to pick up?"

"Sure, can you get me a veggie burger, I haven't eaten yet?"

"Sure, I'll be there shortly."

"Ok, I'll be counting the minutes Mr. White."

Chad adds his request, "Can you put on that sexy nighty you wore for me last time?"

Tammy blushes. "Sure, your wish is my command." She hangs up the phone, quickly jumps in the shower, and puts on the cute nighty.

Shortly after, the doorbell rings, Tammy opens the door and welcomes Chad.

Her beauty causes Chad to become extremely excited. "Hey there sexy." he kisses her cheek and walks through the door.

"Hi handsome." She says as she closes the door and begins kissing him. She guides him to her bedroom where the caressing advances to making love. Chad is working hard to please himself and Tammy.

However Tammy thinks, "Damn, what he's doing isn't pleasing me at all. It sure doesn't compare to the kind of lovin' Sweets provided. All Chad is doing is just a lot of humping and jumping. I can't even feel him inside of me. Did he actually stick it in yet or what, because I sure can't feel a thing. The only thing I can feel is him humping and sweating all over me. I sure hope he doesn't get my hair wet with all this damn sweating, because I just got it done. Just hurry up and get your nut so this can be over." Tammy is totally disappointed. She plays it off as if she's enjoying his company. She fakes the sounds of having an orgasm to rush the occasion. However, the entire time she's thinking of Sweets and how good he made her feel. She moans a few more times to act as if Chad's work isn't in vain.

She whispers, "This is going to be a long night."

Right before Chad was about to cum he said, "What did you say?" However, before she could answer, his goal was achieved and moaning sounds of him cumming are heard.

Surprised by his question, Tammy didn't realize she is talking out loud and quickly responds, "Nothing, I didn't say anything." She looks at him with a confused look and says, "You're done already?" She is disappointed the sex is already over.

He rolls off of her with a big smile on his face. "Yes, and boy did you feel good! It's been almost a year since we've been together. I sure missed you." Chad is feeling proud and content.

With a nonchalant look, Tammy admits, "Yeah, it has been that long."

"I hope it was as good for you as it was for me."

Under her breath she says, "Yeah right."

"What did you say? I didn't hear what you said."

Tammy realizes what she said and again, quickly changes her story. "Oh, yes, it was good for me as well," she said. Then she thinks, "Damn, I wish I would have just waited. These five minute sex acts are not worth my time. Now I know why I haven't talked to Chad in almost a year. Next time I'll just use my dildo. At lease it can keep going until I'm satisfied." She rolls over into his arms to act like everything is alright as he smiles and falls asleep snoring in her ear.

Totally disappointed, Tammy looks at him and shakes her head, "Damn, a wasted night." She quietly gets up to take a shower while he lays asleep in her bed smiling.

Not Quite Good Enough

Seventeen - *Did He Make You Holler?*

"Hey girl, it looks like you didn't get much sleep last night." Cindy pries as Tammy walks into the office looking sleepy.

Tammy's face lights up with the biggest smile. "To tell the truth I didn't. Chad came by and we talked for quite awhile."

Cindy is surprised and smiles back, "Andddd, what else did you two do? Because I know you're horny. So I know you didn't just talk alllll night long. Especially when you had a man in your house who loves the ground you walk on."

"Get out my business busybody." Tammy jokes and picks up a patient's file to act like she's reading it.

"Look who's calling someone a busybody. You're Ms. Busybody number one. Welllll, I'm waiting." With her arms folded, Cindy stands expecting details.

With attempts of deceiving Cindy, Tammy smirks to play the part. "For your information we DID handle our business."

Cindy becomes thrilled while waiting for more details. "Girl, was it good? Did he make you holler?"

"You're crazy! But for your information the only one hollering was him!" Tammy says as they laugh like schoolgirls.
Cindy gives Tammy a high five. "Heyyy! You go girl!"

Tammy can't wait to tell her sorry. She gets serious and said, "Between you and me it wasn't that good at all. It was alright. To be honest, I need more than what Chad can offer. He just can't handle what I need. Hell, I just laid there and let him get his groove on while I waited for him to finish. Girl, he's so small I couldn't even feel him inside of me. But if you ask him, he was getting his groove onnnnn!" They laugh as she continues, "Then, after his five minute marathon was over, I remembered why I hadn't been with him in almost a year. Can you believe that he was done in only five minutes? I just laid there and acted like I was enjoying myself until it was over. I told him everything he wanted to hear in case I get desperate again and need him to return."

Cindy is amazed by what she's hearing, "Damn girl, I feel sorry for you. Especially knowing how horny you are and haven't had any sex since Chad. Well, maybe we need to make appointments with Sweets! I hear he always satisfies the women he's with."

Tammy gets upset. "Don't mention HIS name around me. I'm not sinking THAT low!" A patient comes into the office and the conversation stops.

Tammy suddenly puts on a happy face. "Hi Mrs. Wells. It's good to see you again. I can see you now. Come on back with me."

"Thank you doctor. Good morning Cindy. Nice to see you again." Mrs. Wells walks back to a private room, with Tammy following behind her.

"Good morning Mrs. Wells," Cindy responds. "Nice to see you too." After they are out of sight, Cindy begins daydreaming, "Damn, all this talk about sex has got me horny. I can't wait for my lunch break to have a date with *Buzz Thick*." Cindy knew *Buzz Thick* very well.

While sitting at her desk daydreaming about her lunch break, Cindy smiles. She gets up to make a trip to the restroom to wipe off the lustful lubrication created in her thong underwear. A smiling faced Cindy returns to her desk anticipating the pleasure her lunch break will bring her.

Not Quite Good Enough

Eighteen - *Sexual Pleasures*

It's about seven in the evening when Sweet's' cell phone rings. "Sweets is my name and lovin' is my game!" The handsome and sexy voice said as he answers the phone.

"Hello Sweets." The female voice responds.

"You got em'. Now who is this sweet and sexy voice I'm speaking to?" He asks. He was hoping the mysterious voice would lead to his next quest of sexual pleasure.

"This is Tammy."

Sweets automatically becomes sarcastic, "Ohhh, so this is the lovely doctor who doesn't want anything to do with me." he says. With anger, he continues, "What the hell do you want? I don't have anytime for bullshit!"

Feeling bad, Tammy begins to redeem her actions. "I'm sorry. I was just having a busy day and you called at a bad time. I also told you that I heard you were sharing our sexual business to everyone at the shop. Now THAT, really wasn't cool! Don't you think that would set anybody off?"

In a cool, calm, and confident tone, Sweets defends himself. "Listen here sweet lady, if Sweets takes his time to talk about any of his ladies believe me, it's all good. Otherwise, if you weren't worth talking about, you wouldn't be worth my time. Don't you know there are several ladies who wish I was talking about them. So count yourself as lucky!"

Tammy has a big smile on her face and innocently said. "Ok."

"Now that we cleared that up, so sweet lady, what reason do I get for the pleasure of your phone call?" Sweets is still hoping the call will be a conversation that serves his sexual pleasure and puts more money in his pockets.

"I was thinking about you. I want to see you." She said with a girlish tone.

"Now you're talking. When and where?" Sweets rubs his hands together and smiles.

"Now, at my place."

"Ok, hold tight. I gotta finish this call and I'll see you shortly. Give me about an hour."

"Ok, I'll see you then, bye." They hang up their phones. Tammy happily gets into the shower to prepare for what is to come.

Not Quite Good Enough

Nineteen - *Why Bring Candy to a Candy Store?*

Sophia and Vicki are meeting at a bar. Sophia is sitting at a table waiting when Vicki shows up. "Your hair looks nice. Marque' hooked you up real good."

Vicki models her hairstyle and smiles. "You really like it? I think he did a great job!"

"Yeah girl. You look good!" Sophia pats and admires the new hairdo. "Maybe now I can get a man like you did."

"Oh, so now you want a man?" Sophia asks with a sarcastic and funny tone. "I thought you didn't roll like that."

"Yes I do and what made you think that?"

"Because every time I talk about getting a man you discourage me."

"Sorry!" Vicki quickly changes the subject, "Did you order yet?"

"Yes, I have a beer coming and I ordered one for you." Sophia says.

While eating a hand full of pretzels, Vicki asks, "Good, so how did your date go with Brad?"

Sophia becomes excited and welcomes the conversation, "It went GREAT! We had a really good time. It was nice spending time with a man who didn't look or talk to me like I was his sister or casual friend."

Vicki agrees, "I heard that. So, do you think I can get a man with my new hairdo and look?" She again pats her hair and bats her eyelashes to display the new ones recently added.

"Sure you can. If not here, for sure at the Valentine's Day party. There'll be plenty to choose from."

"I heard that. I have an invitation for you." Vicki pulls out the invitation and gives it to Sophia. The beers arrive.

"Thanks. This should be fun. Maybe I'll invite Brad."

"Forget Brad, why bring candy to a candy store? You might meet someone else."

Sophia shakes her head negatively, "There you go again hatin'."

"I'm not hatin'. I'm just keeping it real."

Sophia changes the subject. "Look, there's a few guys looking at us." She has noticed a few men watching them from across the room and gets excited. "Act like you don't see them."

Vicki becomes excited. "Girllllll, I guess I'll go get my hair and makeup done more often."

They laugh, "Who you telling, me too." They give each other a high five.

The two guys come to their table. "Excuse us ladies, but are you alone?"

They smile and answer together, "Yes!"

The guys smile and respond, "May we sit with you?"

Sophia and Vicki begin blushing to the request and answer together. "Sure." The guys grab a seat and sit down to have a conversation, making Sophia and Vicki feel like they struck gold.

"Hello ladies, how are you tonight?" One of the guys ask.

"We're good, how about you?" Sophia responds.

"Yeah, we're fine." Vicki adds with a big smile.

"My name is Ron." He extends his hand for them to shake.

"Mine is Steve." He also extends his hand.

The ladies are blushing because they're not used to the attention.

"So tell us, are you ladies taken?" Ron asks.

"No." they respond together and giggle like embarrassed schoolgirls.

Steve acknowledges, "We've never seen you in here before. Are you new in the area?" He smiles while admiring Sophia and Vicki, who are drinking their beers.

"We come in here all the time," Vicki responds.

With a surprised look, Ron questions, "You do? We do too. So why haven't we noticed you before now?"

"Maybe because we just stay to ourselves, or maybe you

Not Quite Good Enough

noticed our new hairstyles." Vicki said.

"Yeah, that's it." Sophia adds.

The guys agree and smile as Steve admits, "Yes, your hair does look good. But, we're gonna have to fix the part about you staying to yourselves. You two are definitely somebody we want to see in here more often."

"Yeah, that's right." Ron adds. "We want to see you both much more often." He begins licking his tongue out his mouth, in a seductive way.

"How about us leaving this joint and making some plans of our own?" Steve said.

Vicki and Sophia look at each other, and then they look at the guys and say, "No thank you."

While looking at them, Ron asks with a sarcastic tone, "Why not, it's not like you have anyone else coming to talk to you?" The guys laugh and agree while teasing.

Vicki gets mad. "Oh hell no! We don't even know you guys. You could of at least offered us a drink rather than thinking we're just desperate and horny. Do you think we would jump in the bed with you right away?" she snaps. "Hell, you didn't even ask us our names. Just get away from us," Sophia shakes her head in agreement.

Steve fights back and confesses, "We see you bitches in here all the time and I have to admit the new hairstyles worked wonders for your looks. Ya'll was truly tore up from the floor up before the stylist who did magic on you got to you." The guys agree and laugh. "That's why nobody ever wants to talk to you. We see you leaving alone all the time. So we figured we'd make this your lucky day, by paying you some attention and letting us satisfy you. But forget it! We don't have time for your shit. We're out of here." Steve said as they get up from the table and walk away.

"Good and don't come back because we wouldn't sleep with

you losers if you were the last men on earth. We ain't that damn desperate." Vicki defends both of them.

Sophia agrees with Vicki and jumps in, "Yeah, we don't need either of you anyway." Then she looks at Vicki, "Damn, they were something else weren't they?"

"See, you're the one who's so horny and wanted some dick so bad. So why didn't you go for them when you had your chance?" Vicki asks.

"I'm not that desperate to be disrespected that way. Besides, I think me and Brad may have a chance at a relationship. I don't want to mess things up with him."

"Well, rude dudes like that is why I'll keep my vibrators full of batteries, just so I don't have to hear their damn mouths. Come on, let's go. I'm not in the mood to be bothered anymore tonight." Vicki fumes.

"Yeah, I'm not feeling like being in this place anymore myself. I'm with you tonight." Sophia said. They grab their purses and leave the bar.

On their way to the door two other guys approach them who have just walked in and begin flirting. "Excuse us ladies, leaving so soon?"

"Yes." they respond in unison as they continue walking to their cars with the guys following.

"Wait, slow down. Can we talk to you for a few minutes? My name is Kent and my friend here is Tom. We don't want to hurt you, we just want to talk to you nice ladies." Kent says. Sophia and Vicki stop and listen. Tom stands by listening with a hopeful smile.

"Well, we're not having a very good night here, so we're on our way home." Sophia responds.

"Can we change that mood and talk to you pretty ladies for just a few minutes? We're new here and you ladies look like someone

Not Quite Good Enough

who we'd love to get to know." Tom adds.

Sophia and Vicki look at each other and smile, "Ok, sure, I guess it won't hurt, but just a few minutes." Vicki said.

"Ok, great." Kent says and continues. "Come on, lets go back inside." He gestures for all of them to return back inside the bar. "Can we buy you a drink and also ask what your names are?"

Sophia looks at Vicki to see what she is thinking. With a nod of approval, they agree. "Sure, that'll be fine. My name is Vicki and her name is Sophia." Vicki said. They walk back into the bar smiling, sit at a table to order beers, and enjoy a nice long conversation with Kent and Tom. Steve and Ron standing alone, jealously eyeing them from across the room.

After a few hours of pleasant conversation, Sophia and Vicki call it a night and decide to leave. Kent and Tom walk each of them to their separate cars and give them their telephone numbers.

T' La June

Twenty - *The Booty Call*

    Tammy stands in front of the mirror admiring her slender and sexy curves while she awaits her booty call. It was just the day before when Tammy had sex with Chad. Since she was totally disappointed by Chad's performance, she still lacked some good lovin' and knew Sweet would not disappoint her. Therefore, she happily awaited Sweets' arrival. She sprays a seductive spray of perfume over herself and inhales the fragrance. She devilishly smiles, thinking of how he acts when he smells the fragrance, as the doorbell rings. With one last pat of her flowing hair she opens the door greeting her visitor with a sultry tone and smile. "Hi there, glad you could make it with such a short notice." She stands at the door looking sexy with her long, silk, laced black negligee and under a slinky see-through robe.

    Once Sweets sees her, he grins and shows all his teeth. "You ring baby, I come singing! So, what can sweet daddy do for you tonight?" He walks into her luxury condo.

    Without saying a word, Tammy is still smiling and thinks, "Anything he wants to do is fine with me." She closes the front door, begins kissing Sweets while leading him straight to her bedroom. She pushes him to her bed and jumps in his lap.

    "So I see you're ready for some more of my good and plenty lovin'?"

"Yes of course I'm ready."

    Tammy is kissing his neck when suddenly he stops her, pushes her away, and gives her a piece of his mind in a stern tone. "First of all we have to get something straight. Don't ever talk to me with that bullshit attitude, or hang up in my face like you did the other day when you were at work. Baby, I'm Sweets and I don't put up with that kinda shit from any bitch, and Frank sure doesn't either! We go back too damn far for you to be giving me all your shit! If you don't want your reputation to be ruined then cut out the bullshit! I'm serious about that shit, do you understand me?" Tammy's high-class status didn't mean a thing to him. Sweets is determined to let her know the cards were now in his favor.

Suddenly Tammy's good mood changes to sad and shame, "Damn Frank, why did you have to go there? I thought tonight was going to be about love and not war. We ended the war years ago. So what's your damn problem now?" She gets up and walks away from him and goes to the other side of the room feeling bad.

"You're my damn problem." He gets up and walks closer, getting in her face. "Doing all that smart-ass talking ain't gonna fly with me. I know you don't want the word to get out that we have a sixteen year old daughter named Danielle, do you?"

Surprised by his admission, Tammy becomes scared that her secret skeleton is revealed. "How did you find that out?"

"You forget we come from the same small town and the people who live in it love to spread gossip, and stay in other folks' business. Besides, I still have a few faithful friends back home that I visit every once in awhile. So I see and hear things for my damn self. I've known for years that your momma is raising our child. So, what's it gonna be? Are we gonna keep the peace and make love or war? You decide."

Tammy is surprised by Sweets' confession and begins buttering him up with her love. "I called you here to make love. You know I could never get enough of your good lovin' when we were young and after the other night, I'm hooked again." She tries to change the mood. "I was so glad to hear you moved here. I'd been looking for you for a long time. I just couldn't tell anyone about you. When you left us, you broke my heart. I didn't think I would ever forgive you. But we were young and that's in the past. Now, all I want to feel is the entire shaft of your masculinity inside of me. I wanna holler and scream like I did the last time you were here. Nobody can ever make me feel as good as you. So, let's stop all the talking and get to making love." She begins kissing his neck and caressing his penis with her hand, trying to turn him on and change the subject, knowing her good reputation was on the line if her skeleton was revealed.

Sweets smiles from the tempting feelings going through his body as her hands caress his treasured possession. Yet he attempts to resist her soft fingers stroking his manhood while he explains his past. "Look, I understand that you were upset, but I had to leave town. I had a contract out on my life and I couldn't let anyone know where I was, not even my own mother. I couldn't risk getting anyone else involved in some shit I got myself in. I had to handle things on my own or I was going to get killed along with the people who were in my life. The brotha who was after me went to jail and so did his boyz. So it's all good now."

"Good, so let's make love right now." Tammy continues caressing his body.

Sweets is smiling, but still trying to explain while trying to hold back his excitement. "Wait baby, let me finish," he hesitantly whispers while her fully-opened mouth journeys down South as she reaches the head of his masculinity and enjoys it's pleasures.

"I'm listening, go ahead." She said while her head bobs up and down, creating a pleasurable moment for both of them. Later she allows her tongue to journey up his body, massaging his powerful six pack abdomen, and while still fondling his masculinity with her hands; causing it to remain to heights of extreme intense.

Sweets is smiling while luring her head up toward his as he looks into her eyes, "Baby listen, one day I want to meet my daughter. I want her to know that I am her daddy, just like all the other kid's." Then he kisses her and massages her breast while sampling every inch with his tongue.

Not Quite Good Enough

Suddenly the mood changes and Tammy stops in her tracks, she backs away from him and asks bluntly, "The other kid's? What do you mean, the other kid's?" She says surprised. "Just how many damn kids do you have?"

"Nine, which includes ours."

She gets up and walks away from him. "NINE? Damn Frank, you've been a screwing bastard haven't you?" In a sarcastic and angry tone she continues. "So tell me, are you taking care of all of them? Or did you run away from them like your daddy did to you and your six brothers and sisters?"

"Hell no, I haven't ran away from any of my kids." He said angrily. "I just put them on hold for a minute while I got my shit together, that's all. I've seen a few of them since I came out of hiding. That's why I want to meet the kid I had with you. As soon as things really get rolling for me, I'll be able to take care of them. For now, their momma's take care of them. If not, then the county provides their needs. Like I said earlier, I didn't want anyone to get hurt with the mess I was in, let alone killed. So I stayed away from everybody. But I'm good now."

"Damn Sweets, nine babies? That's some crazy shit."

"I know it is." He begins caressing her breast and kissing her neck. She starts to melt back into his arms. He continues to say, "I can't help it if the women I've been with didn't use protection. Shit, I hate putting on rain coats. I like to feel the real deal. Hell, I only started using them because no one protected themselves. I got tired of women coming up to me years later, telling me that I was their babies daddy. I also didn't want to get infected with HIV. But all that's water under the bridge. Now I want each of my kids to know who their daddy is and that he loves them. I also want them to know who their other brothers and sisters are so we can all be family."

Tammy begins to sympathize with him. "Well, just let me

know when you're ready to meet Danielle and I'll make sure you do." Then she pleads her case with him. "Now, as far as me and you are concerned, I just want you to keep anything we do together our secret, including our child. That's all I want and we'll be fine."

Sweets takes her hands, smiles, and looks deep into her eyes. "Suga', I have no problem with that request. I ain't tripping. But don't be starting no shit with me," He jokes and kisses her lips. "Now, let me give you some of this good lovin' because I know that white guy you've been with can't touch Sweets good lovin'! So, come here girl."

Tammy is again surprised by his confession. "Damn Frank, what else do you know about me? I see you've been keeping close tabs on what I've been doing."

He smiles, "You'll never know." Then he gets a serious look on his face. "So don't ever fuck with me! And call me Sweets! The name Frank died after I left home and had to be on the run for my life!"

Tammy smiles, "Ok, Sweets."

They start kissing and begin to make love. They both begin to undress each other and begin making love. "Oh Sweets, Oh Sweets. You're the best lover I've ever had."

"And don't you ever forget that shit." He aggressively rocks her world up and down, in ways only he could perform. The more they make love, the more they sweat, and passionately moan.

"Damn girl, you're better today than you were last week, what's up? You're making me work harder and I'm enjoying every bit of this ride! You go girl!" Sweets continues to get his groove on as Tammy strokes his body with all her might, making sure to get more than five minutes of fun.

"Hell, it's been a whole week and I was horny." She lies, knowing she was just with Chad yesterday, and continues. "So a girl's got to do what a girl's got to do in order to get her groove on," she says

Not Quite Good Enough

while getting the ride of her life.

"Well let's get it on with your bad self, because I'm surely not complaining. Ride' em' cowgirl! Yeeee haaaa!" Their lovemaking escalates, becoming wilder, making the headboard repeatedly bang against the wall.

Tammy is moaning. "Ummmmm, Ahhhhh! Oh yeah, you're making me feel real good tonight. I'm really getting my groove on!"

"Well get it on girl!"

With all the lovemaking going on, the headboard continues to beat on the adjacent wall when suddenly the neighbors began yelling and beating on the wall. "Hey, keep it down over there! We got kids in here!" Tammy and Sweets smile and continue making love without buying into the interruptions.

"Ummmm, yeahhhh! I feel sooo good. I'm cummingggggg!" Tammy yells as she reaches new heights.

"Cum on Suga', cum for Sweet Daddy!" Sweets smiles and watches Tammy's body burst with excitement.

"Call my name, call my name!" He tells her.

She yells, "Sweets, Sweetsssssss!!" until she cums at the same time as him.

"Ahhhhhh!" They both beam while their bodies vibrate with total satisfaction.

T' La June

Twenty-One - *Sexual Delight*

It's eight in the morning and Marque' is waking up next to his male lover moving in slow motion. "Damn I don't want to get up today." Then his tone becomes sensual as he twirls the curls of his lovers hair through his fingers. "Tommy Boy you put it on me good last night. I'm still feeling you inside of me. Lets have a quicky before I go to work."

Billy smiles, "Anything you say. I got nothing but time to share my good thang with you baby!" Marque' and Billy kiss and begin to again make love.

"Damn Billy Boy, you do know how to rock my world, yeahhhh!" Marque' said as they kiss, rub and stroke each other's body.

"Marque', you're my bitch. I'm always gonna make you happy!" Billy continues in the passion.

"Oh shit, oh shit, I'm cumming, damnnnnnnnn!" Marque' groans as his body explodes. Billy continues to stroke Marque's naked body while passionately kissing him and making him feel satisfied and happy.

Marque' returns the favor of satisfaction until it's Billy's turn to climax. "Ohhhhhhhh!! Ohhhhhhhhhh!!! He too explodes into a sexual delight.

Marque kisses Billy before rolling over to look at the clock. He notices it's 9am. "Damn, now I better get going before I'm late for my first appointment. Come take a shower with me."

Billy smiles, "Ok, you get in and I'll join you after I pee and turn on the coffee pot."

With a naughty boy look on his face Marque' said, "You can pee on me." They kiss and smile.

Billy blushes, "You nasty boy, I love you. But let me turn on the coffee pot before I get in. Then you can pee on me all you want."

Not Quite Good Enough

he jokes.

"I'll be waiting, so don't take too long."

While Marque' is taking his shower, Billy sneaks up on him and throws a bucket of ice cold water, with ice cubes, over the top of the shower door onto Marque', causing him to scream like a girl. "Ahhhhh! You bitch! I'm gonna get you. Come back here." Marque' screams as he runs butt naked out the shower chasing Billy. Once he caught Billy, they laugh together, kiss, and jump in the shower. Afterwards they get dressed and leave for work.

T' La June

Twenty-Two - *The Three-Some*

It's 9:45 AM and Mae May has just opened the shop. Marque follows shortly after with a huge smile on his face. "Good-morningggg!!!"

Mae May looks at Marque' strangely. "Why are you coming in here with that big ass grin on your face?"

"If you have to ask you don't need to know."

Mae May laughs, "You and Billy act like damn rabbits. You screw every chance you get!" Then Mae May sticks out her butt and shakes it toward Marque' as they laugh.

"Don't be a hater, be a lover!" Marque chirps back.

"I ain't hating all that much bitch because I got me some dick too last night."

"Well, well, well! Tell bitch, tell." Marque' says as he sits down at Mae May's manicure station and continues. "So, who rocked your world last night and made you feel lucky inside? I want the who, what, when, and where of who screwed you? Because I know you can't bring no one to your house with all those bad ass kids you got, and with your drunk ass momma listening to everything, other than your kids, that moves in that house."

Mae May burst out laughing, "Oh, so you're a comedian today? That's alright, I can handle it. Bring it on!"

Marque' laughs and says, "Girl you know I love you. So tell me, who laid you last night? Come on, who's the lucky man or woman? I want details. You know I love gossip, come on with it."

"Sweets!" Mae May brags and yells. "Helllll Yeahhhhhhh!!! I got me some more of Sweets' hot ass dick last night and it was finger lickin' good!" She licks her fingers to demonstrate and continues. "Um, um, ummmmm!" Pretending she is humping the air.

Marque' smiles with a surprised and jealous look on his face,

Not Quite Good Enough

"Damn, how'd you pull that shit off? Remember, I thought he said he wouldn't be with you again. Bitch I was waiting for him for my own damn self. How did you get his tight sexy ass between your legs again?"

Mae May is beaming, "Yeah, yeah, yeah! A brotha will tell you anything until you put your legs up in his face and show him what you're working with." Mae May erotically dips her hips while holding on to the back of her chair, and shakes her butt in the air like she's doing a pole dance move.

"You bitch! You did that?"

Proud of her accomplishment, Mae May continues bragging. "You better believe it. Shitttt, after seeing him the other night, I had to get me some more."

Marque' gets up from his chair and becomes more excited. "Tell me more!"

Mae May is laughing from Marque's impatient actions, "Calm down doggy, calm down. Anyway, after the club let out, I went over to Cindy's house so we could get high and Sweets followed us. After a few hits we were having hot fun in the summer time, all three of us! Heyyy!"

"You hoe!" Marque' says waiting for more details. "Go on, tell more."

"Excuse me? Please correct yourself because a hoe get's paid, but we got laid! And it sure was good! Heyyyyyy!!!" Mae May teases with pride.

"Damn!" Marque' shakes his head in disbelief and continues. "Wait a minute, I don't think I heard you correctly. You mean Ms. Prissy-Ass Cindy, who thinks she's better than everyone else and too good for most brothas around here, did a three-some with you and Sweets last night?"

"Hell yeah, that Cindy."

"Damnnnn! And I thought Cindy was sweet and innocent."

T' La June

"She sure was sweet when me and Sweets was eating her last night!" Mae May licks her lips in a circular motion and sucks on her middle finger. "Her innocence turned us the hell onnnnnn!"

"Oh, so now I see, she's a closet hoe." Marque' and Mae May laugh uncontrollably as Marque' continues. "You bitches. Why didn't you invite me? You know I want to taste Sweets' tootsie roll too. Hell I've been wanting to taste him for years." he confesses.

"Yeah, yeah, yeah, I know you do! But you didn't and you never will." She flaunts and continues. "But I'm here to tell you that Sweets tasted damn good last night. All eight inches of him. Lord have mercy!" Mae May waves her hands in the air.

"Well excuse the hell outta me. I ain't mad at ya! But I want MORE details."

Mae May is happy to continue her story. "Ok, here's how it went. Cindy and I went to a club. Right before the club closed we saw Sweets standing outside. So we went over to him and started talking. The next thing you know he followed us to Cindy's house, because you know I couldn't take him to my house. We got high and the rest is GREAT fucking ass history!" Mae May brags.

"Damn, damn, damnnnn!" Marque' jokingly pouts.

"But wait, this was funny." She continues, "Even though it wasn't funny when the shit happened." Marque' is glued to every word coming out of her mouth as she continues. "While we were getting our groove on I was massaging my hands in Sweets' and Cindy's hair when, hold on, I gotta go pee." Mae May stops telling her story to run to the restroom.

"Pee? Oh hell no. Bitch, you can't stop right in the middle of telling a juicy story about screwing Sweets and just stop. Hell, pee later and tell me the rest NOW! So, what happened?" Marque' begs, giving Mae May his undivided attention..

Mae May turns back around and continues, "Okkkk bitch,

hold your horses. So, it went like this; It was about 3 in the morning when me, Cindy, and Sweets are in the heat of our sex-capade. Then all of a sudden the romantic mood changes."

What? What happened?" Marque' pleads.

"I'm getting to it, hold on. Ok, where was I?"

"You guys were enjoying a sex-capade. Then what?" Marque' guides Mae May's story.

"Oh yeah, we were getting our groove onnn, until Sweet's condom broke."

Marque' is blown away with what he's hearing. "Get the hell out of here, his condom broke? Oh shit! That shit ain't funny. Go ahead, continue." Marque' said.

With one hand on her hip, the other waving around in the air, and her neck rolling, Mae May's attitude is expressing itself in body language. "Yeah, that's what we thought because you know Sweets is a hoe to the 10th power. I sure don't want to get any diseases from his ass. You feel me?"

"I feel ya." Marque' answers. "So what did you do?"

Mae May continues, "Well, the sex was soooo good we didn't notice his condom had come off. He had been screwing me and Cindy at the same time. He was putting his dick in me for a few minutes, then putting it in Cindy for a few minutes, back and forth, in and out. Then after he came, he looked down and noticed it was off. Soooo, none of us knew how long it had actually been off."

"Damnnnn!"

Mae May continues, "Anyway, he got up, wiped the juices off him, and said he was sorry. We didn't care. All we cared about at that time was getting some lovin' from Sweets. Then we stroked his dick with our hands to get him hard again, gave him some more head, and got to screwing again! This time without the condom on purpose."

"Damnnn, I sure hope you hoe's don't get pregnant." Marque' notes.

"Yeah tell me about it, because I get pregnant by someone just looking at me too long. But I should be alright, I'm on the pill." Mae May said with confidence then thinks, "Oh shit,"

"What?" Marque' questions then says. "You have been taking your pills, right?"

"I forgot to pick up my last order from the pharmacy. I forgot I haven't taken them in the last few days. Damn, I sure hope I don't get pregnant, damnnnn!!"

"I sure hope you don't either because that would make five babies for you girl. Which means you really are a hoe to the 5th power!" Marque' jokes.

"Funny. Ha, ha, ha, my ass! Anyway, let me finish." Mae May remarks before going on. "Then, everything was going strong again. We were all having a damn good time when all of sudden my nail broke. So I said, 'Oh shit, my nail broke! Wait, be still I told Cindy because I figured it was stuck in her weave. So Sweets and Cindy stop screwing. I was tripping so hard, looking for it that Cindy began helping me look for my broken nail inside her weave."

"Damnnn. I can't believe you left that sweet brown thang laying on the bed alone while you looked for a damn fingernail."

"Well, I did." Mae May says and continues. "Shut up and listen." Marque' listens and May Continues. "Anyway, I didn't look up right away to notice that Sweets was holding his eye until he yelled. 'Damn you Mae May, your nail didn't go in her weave, that shit hit me in my eye. You're about to scratch out my damn eye with those long ass nails.'" Sweets yells.

"So I looked at Sweets with an attitude and said, 'Forget your damn eye. I gotta find my nail. Its taken me too damn long to grow these things."

"Mae May, I can't believe it took you that long to find one long ass, shiny, rhinestone, multi-colored fingernail. Damn. Now you're

Not Quite Good Enough

making ME mad. Go on, what happened next?" Marque' said while still being glued to every word.

"Ok, listen and keep your two cent to yourself, or I'm not gonna finish my story." Mae May warns. Marque' shakes his head to agree before Mae May continues. "Then Cindy said, 'Mae May, you're spoiling the mood with your damn nail. We're supposed to be screwing all this thickness aiming for our attention. Hurry up.' So I looked at her and said, that's too bad, the mood will come back after I find my nail. If you didn't have this long multi-colored shag carpet I would have found it awhile ago. I sure hope you have some nail glue because I left mine at home, and I can't be seen without my long nails. Soon after, Cindy ignores me, gets on her knees and starts giving Sweets head while I continued looking. Sweets then looks down at me because my head gets in their way and says, 'Girl, forget being seen without your long ass tiger claw nails. I'll tell you what, you better fix your nail before it cuts out my entire eye or scratches my pretty face, or no more of my good and plenty lovin for you. You see, I can't mess up what helps me pay my bills.'"

"Damn, all this for a damn fingernail when you had a big thick joy stick in front of your face? Damn Mae May, didn't I teach you better than that?" Marque' questions with humor.

"Yeah, yeah, yeah! Whateverrrr! Let me finish." Mae May says and continues. "So anyway, Cindy gets back on the floor and continues helping me. Suddenly Sweets attitude changes when he notices our naked butts raised high in the air, exposing everything, while searching. So he sits up straight and admires the view and begins smiling and licking his lips and says. 'Yeah, that's it, keep that position rightttt there! Ummmmm!!! Take your time.' he says. Then he begins to satisfy himself by jacking off until he almost came while watching us."

"Damnnnnn bitch, I still can't believe you didn't call me! And you let him jack off, alone, while you bitches looked for a damn fingernail? Oh hell no! That was definitely a waste of cum. I really could have taken care of that situation in a better way than THAT! Believe me, if I was there, his cum wouldn't have gone to waste." Marque' said upset. "I'm gonna pay your ass back big time for this one. Go ahead, finish!"

"No, he didn't cum, he almost did. Anyway, Cindy was getting impatient and said, 'Hurry up Mae May before the mood is totally gone. It was bad enough the mood was lost when Sweets' condom broke."

"Oh yeah, I'm with Cindy, that mood was definitely gone. So what did you guys do then?"

"Well, we stopped him from cumming and went back to screwing, that's what we did." Mae May jokes
"You kept screwing without the condom?"

"Hell yeah. You mean to tell me that if that shit happened to you, you would have stopped screwing Sweets just because his condom broke and he didn't have an extra one?"
"Hell no!" Marque' says.
"So I guess you understand my point then."

Marque' continues, "But shittt, if the joy stick was as good as you say it is, then it would have felt better without one anyway."

"My point exactly. So let me finish my damn story and quit interrupting me." Marque' shakes his head and smiles as Mae May continues. "Anyway, we were looking for my nail. Cindy was mad as hell so she told me to hurry up and find it so we could get back to our business. I did, and the rest of our time was just fine, without any interruptions."

"So what was Sweets doing while ya'll was looking for your nail?"

"Sitting there watching us, stroking himself to keep content. Hell, he was too high to do anything else. He knew he wasn't going

Not Quite Good Enough

anywhere anytime soon anyway. Later he had the nerve to say, 'I also gotta remember to get some better condoms. I can't keep having this shit happen. These jimmy's ain't large enough for me. I need the ultra super, super size.'"

Marque' said, "Damnnnnnnnnn!! Now I know I want a piece of Sweets' sweets if the damn large condoms are too small. All I gotta do is get him super high. Damnnnnnnn, I could have taken care of that a long time ago." Marque' proceeds, "Damnnnnnn. Ok bitch, I'm gonna tell you this one last time. You bitches should have called my horny ass. I would have made SURE Sweets was well taken care of while you bitches looked for a damn nail. I would have said forget that nail, give me Sweets. Damnnnnn I hate ya'll didn't call me!" Mae May laughs as Marque' finishes. "Next time you better call me bitch or I'ma jack you up!"

"I will bitch." Mae May said. She continues, "But keep that info to yourself. Cindy doesn't want Tammy to know she screwed Sweets."

"Why? If Sweets' shit is so damn good why wouldn't someone want to kiss and tell that they had a taste of his good and plenty?" Marque' questions.

"You know how Tammy is. All she thinks about is getting a man with money. If she knew Cindy had sex with Sweets, she would just tell her that she's too good for him. Cindy doesn't feel like hearing all that. Since Cindy and Tammy are best friends, Tammy is always telling Cindy to get a man with money like her. When she tries to date a man without a job or someone who has a low paying job Tammy always trips. You know how Cindy is, Ms. Secret hoe, always wanting everyone to believe she's a good girl. She's also always trying to please her skinny-ass boss Tammy. In fact, last night Cindy was going to pass up our sex-capade with Sweets because she was thinking about what Tammy would say if she found out. I hate meddling skinny bitches like Tammy. They always think they know every damn thang. Anyway, I told Cindy she better please herself and quit worrying about pleasing Tammy. I also told her that Tammy couldn't please her the way Sweets would please both of us. So she joined in."

"Damn, damn, damn! I ain't gonna say it one more time, next time you bitches better invite me. Then, get Sweets super high so he won't know it's me sucking on him. I know he doesn't roll like that, but hell if I care. All I care about is getting a piece of his sweet thang. Although, after I got done with him, and he realizes how good I'll make his feel, he might change his mind." They laugh and change the conversation when a customer walks in the shop.

Not Quite Good Enough

Twenty-Three - *He Can't Please me*

Tammy and Cindy are opening the office when Cindy questions Tammy. "What did you do last night?"

Tammy is caught off guard by the question. She secretly thinks about Sweets and answers. "Watched TV," she grins and continues. "I was so tired I didn't want to do anything else."

Cindy also thinks about what she did last night with Sweets and Mae May. As she willingly lies to Tammy, "me too."

While looking through patients' charts, Tammy begins to daydream about her night with Sweets. "Damn the sex was damn good last night! Since I've been back with Sweets, it has been the best sex I've had in a very long time. I miss being with him."

"You mean Chad didn't call you again last night?"

"What did you say?" Tammy's thoughts are suddenly distracted as Cindy continues to ask questions.

"I said, didn't Chad call you again last night?" She repeats while opening the mail. She wasn't really concerned with Tammy's answer since she's still reminiscing her own thoughts.

Tammy's good mood suddenly changes which gets Cindy's full attention. Tammy yells, "Hell no he didn't call. I don't want him to call me again. In fact, I don't want anything to do with him ever again. He can't please me sexually and he just lost his job. So what do I need him for? I need to find a man who can spend money on me and not expect me to spend all my money on him. I'll just wait for the Valentine's Day party to find a good man. Since there'll be five other salons joining, maybe I'll get lucky then. You know Marque's acquainted with all kinds of brothas'. Who knows what other brothas', will be attending from the other salons. I can't wait." Tammy smiles at the thought.

"Me either. I just hope some straight brothas' come."

Because you know what kind of crowd Marque' draws," Cindy said as they laugh.

"So true. But he told me he would make sure to have some nice guys attend for us single and straight girls."

"I sure hope so," Cindy adds before changing the subject. "Well, the other night I met this guy on the internet. He sounded pretty cool. He said his name was Brad. The picture he had in his profile page was hard to see so I told him about the party. He said, he would come. I figure this way if I don't like him, I can just lose him in the crowd."

"That's what I'm talking about." They laugh, give each other a fist bump and go to work; as patients begin to come inside the office.

After Cindy checks in the patients, the office gets quiet. During that time, she begins to smile while daydreaming. "Ummm, I can still feel Sweets inside of me from last night. Damnnn was he good! He was better than I heard or could have ever imagined. In fact, he's the best I've ever had sexually. Damnnnn, that man has super-hero powers! I can see why women pay so much money just to spend their nights with him. Thank God for freebies. I sure can't afford his cute ass. Hell, I need a raise just to be able to afford one night with him. I guess that's how he attracts more women, by letting them sample a taste of what he's got to offer, then you're hooked like a drug! Damnnn! After one night with him, you want more and more, just like a crack addict." Cindy shakes her head while thinking about Sweets. "Shit, after last night, I'll need to take my morning, lunch, and evening breaks in the backseat of my car with my private little buzzing toy, *Buzz Thick*. Hell, I'll have to spend more nights with *Buzz Thick* until I find a man who can rock my world like Sweets. After all the good sex we had last night, it's gonna be hard for another man to fill his big thick chocolate boots. Ummm, ummm, ummm!" She licks her lips as her thoughts lust for more of Sweets.

Not Quite Good Enough

"Cindy, Cindyyyy!" Tammy says while looking at Cindy with a strange look.

"I'm sorry, I was daydreaming." Cindy begins smiling with a stupid grin.

"Yeah, I can see that." Tammy looks at her strangely again. She passes her the file that she needs her to handle. "Please set up a surgery appointment for Mrs. Flowers. Cindy, can you please focus on what you're doing and quit daydreaming?"

"Yes. I'm sorry." Taking the file from Tammy, Cindy goes back to work. "Hi Mrs. Flowers, I'll be right with you."

"No problem. I don't have anywhere to go after my appointment anyway. Take your time Cindy. I'll just sit over there." Mrs. Flowers says and then goes to sit down.

Tammy walks back by Cindy's desk and whispers, "Are you alright? You've been acting strange ever since you came in today. Plus, even when you return from your lunch break. Is everything ok?"

"Yeah, everything's cool. I just have a lot of things on my mind. You know, I'm just taking care of some business. That's all, but I'm good. Thanks for asking." Cindy said as she looks on the computer for an appointment time.

Tammy looks at Cindy strangely. "Ok, if you say so." Tammy then goes to another room to help a patient.

T' La June

Twenty-Four - *Better Than a Dildo*

Vicki walks into her apartment after a long day at work. She is feeling tired when her phone rings. "Hello." She said as she lays down her purse and keys.
"Hey girl, what are you doing?" Sophia asks.
"I just walked in the door from a crazy day at work. Thank God I'm home." Vicki says while taking off her shoes.
"What happened?"
"Those damn women at work make me sick. I get sooo tired listening to their problems, especially when they're the ones who causes them. But you can't get them to believe that they are the problem. They love playing the victim, blaming everyone else for their problems. Hell, I'm the one who's paid big bucks to analyze folks, so why won't they listen to me?"
"Damnnn, what happened?" Sophia grills.
"I keep trying to tell them why their husbands are messing around on them, but they don't want to listen to me. Instead they just complain all the damn time about guys being no good. One of the girls' husband told her that he wants a divorce. Instead of listening to me, they complain all the damn time about the guys being no good."
"Well, most of them are no good, aren't they?" Sophia questions.
"Yeah most of them are, but in their case they're the ones who's wrong."
"How so?"
"Ok think about this and tell me if they're wrong."
"I'm listening." Sophia prepares for the story.
"Ok, if you were a man, who had worked hard all day long, and when you came home you'd find your wife in bed watching television sporting a head rag, eating fast food, and no dinner, would you like it? But wait, before you answer I have another one. Ok, on your

off days, your husband wants to spend time with you but you tell him no. You say going to church and doing favors for your friends come first. Also you don't have time, nor do you care about the things he's interested in doing. Or, every time he wants to make love to you, you tell him you have a headache and don't want to be bothered. So, would you like that?"

Sophia gets ready to answer but Vicki stops her. "Wait, don't answer yet. Here's another good one. Ok, if each week you use your entire paycheck to buy new clothes, get your hair and nails done, buy new things for the house, and the kids, but never think about what your husband needs. Or your husband tells you that his hours have been cut from work, and may be cut again. He tells you that you need to stop spending so much money, and you tell him hell no, that's HIS problem to worry about and not yours. Now tell me, what kind of ignorant bitch spends the money she would use to pay her mortgage on unnecessary shit for the house instead of taking care of her own business? To me, that sounds like someone who wants themselves, the kids, and their house to look good, while she's left out in the cold because her house was put up for auction. Then have the nerve to look at her husband as if the whole mess was his fault and responsibility. So tell me, would you stay with your wife, or not mess around on her? So really, tell me, am I tripping or what?" Vicki was getting everything off her chest, by venting to Sophia.

"Hell no! I'd be gone my damn self with all that going on." Sophia adds.

"That's exactly my point! I tried to tell those dumb girls, but they won't listen to me, and I don't even have a man. What I do know is to not be THAT stupid. Then they wonder why they can't keep their men."

"I agree with you on that one." Sophia admits.

"Girllll, sometimes I wonder who's the real client; those

coming into the center, or those working inside." Vicki responds shaking her head and continues. "So, enough about my day, what's going on with you?"

Sophia becomes excited, ready to share her story. "I was waiting for you to come home. So tell me, what did you think of Tom and Kent?" Sophia asks as she runs through the house changing her clothes.

Vicki begins blushing like a schoolgirl, "I thought a lot about Kent. We actually got together at my house after Tom walked you to your car."

Sophia is surprised by her answer. "You screwed him that quick? You just met him."

"Andddd, what does that have to do with anything?" Vicki snaps back.

"I just asked. But you don't even know him," Sophia replies.

"No I don't, but I'm a grown ass woman who can make her own decisions. Besides, I'm the one who has to live with the decisions I make, no one else. I'll tell you this, the decision to screw him felt pretty damn good. You know, I haven't been with a man in a long time. I was well overdue for some lovin'. I have to admit he felt much better than my trusty-dusty dildo. But hey, when that's all you have, that's all you have." they laugh.

"Damn girl, and you were talking about me wanting to get with a man. Look at you? You beat me to some dick. I'm scared of you missy!" they giggle.

Vicki teases, "Don't be hatin' because you didn't get some dick last night."

"That's alright, I have tonight," Sophia brags.

"What you talking about?"

Suddenly Sophia hears her doorbell ring. "That's Brad. I gotta go!"

Vicki is surprised by her answer and starts laughing, "You

Not Quite Good Enough

Bitch! Goodnight! Have fun and get in a screw or two for me too."

"I plan on it. See ya!" Sophia says as she hangs up the phone. She answers the door with Brad standing there smiling. He is holding a bouquet of yellow roses.

"Wow, you look beautiful!" He gives her a kiss causing her to blush.

"Thank you." Sophia beams. "Thank you for the roses. I haven't had any of these in a long time." She takes the arrangement and sits the bouquet on her kitchen counter.

"Are you ready?" Brad asks.

"Yes, let me get my purse."

Before Sophia leaves the room, Brad gracefully takes her hand, looks deep into her eyes and says, "Don't take too long, I've been thinking about our date all day long." He gently kisses her soft lips which leaves her bashfully blushing. Then he slowly releases her hands while she goes to her bedroom. She feels like the luckiest women in the world.

After getting her purse, Sophia returns to the mirror to make sure everything looks good. She sprays on an extra mist of perfume and walks into the living room where Brad is patiently awaiting her arrival.

He opens the front door in a gentleman's fashion, allowing her to walk out and lock it. Together, they walk to the car where he opens the door for her entry. Both feeling pleasantly happy, they take off to a fancy seafood and steak restaurant in Beverly Hills.

T' La June

Twenty-Five - *Bad-Ass Kids*

Mae May has just come home from work and walks into a quiet house. Emma Jean, her mother is watching TV. After a long and tiring day at work, Mae May appreciates coming home to a quiet house. Mae May walks over to her mother and gives her a kiss on the forehead. "Hey Momma, how was your day?" She looks around the house waiting for her kids to come running to her. "Where's the kids?"

"Hey Baby. Those damn kids were making so much noise I couldn't hear my TV show. So I made their bad asses go to sleep."

Mae May is surprised her mother got all the kids to sleep and asks. "How did you get all four of them to go to sleep so early?"

Emma Jean continues looking at TV, never taking her eyes away from her program. Then with a delayed reaction, she nonchalantly answers, "I gave them a bottle with some beer in it."

Mae May furiously yells, "Momma? You gave them beer?"

Still with a nonchalant tone, Emma Jean defends herself by responding, "Yeah, ain't nothing wrong with a little beer every now and again. Besides, it ain't the first time they've had beer. Their bad asses like beer. They're always trying to drink from my bottle. So I pour it in their bottle's so they don't get slobber in mine. Hell, I used to give it to you all the time when you were their age." Emma Jean looks at Mae May and continues, "Why do you think you like beer so much?" Mae May shakes her head.

"I can't believe you give those kids beer. Damn Momma they don't need to be drinking." She storms out the room and goes to the kid's room where she finds them sound asleep. Their baby bottles are half full of beer and ice cubes just laying there, dripping on their sheets.

Upset, Mae May storms back into the living room where her mom is and says, "Momma, why do they have ice cubes in their bottles

Not Quite Good Enough

WITH the beer?"

While not taking her eyes off the television set, Emma Jean responds. She didn't care what Mae May thought of her decision. "They wanted their beer to be ice cold."

"Damn, you're trying to make them alcoholics just like you before they even get in elementary school." She turns to walk away, but her mother's yell stop her in her tracks.

"Like me? What you mean, just like me?"

"Momma, admit it, you're an alcoholic and you need to stop drinking your life away."

"Drinking my life away? Hell, maybe if I didn't have to take care of your bad-ass kids I wouldn't need to drink. Those bad-ass kids will drive anyone to a drink. You got your damn nerve, you weed head. So don't criticize me." She said in a stern tone. "At least what I do is legal. So Mae May, don't start that shit with me now. I done had a long day. Your kids drive me crazy most of the time, today was especially one of those days."

"Yeah, alright." Mae May says to dispute the theory and continues. "Momma, please don't give them anymore beer."

"Mae May quit all that damn talking, I'm trying to watch my show." Mae May, feeling frustrated, shakes her head again, goes to her bedroom, and slams the door.

T' La June

Twenty-Six - *Sexual Gadgets*

Mae May and Marque' are in the *Lotion in Motion erotic* store looking for sex gadgets for their big Valentine's party. Something special catches Marque's eye, "Girllll, come over here and look at these mini dick and titty key chains. They look yummy. These would be great party favors. Don't you think so?"

Mae May picks up a package of each and admires them. "Girl yeah, they're cute." Mae May admits. "Let's get at least a hundred of em'. I think they'll look great on the tables." She gathers as many as she can find to add to her count.

"We also need to get a large box of condoms in case someone slips into the broom closet or restroom stalls." Marque' said as they both agree at the thought. Marque' grabs several boxes of condoms, in a variety of sizes, and places them in his basket. Mae May has walked away, looking at other items in the store.

Mae May stops a few isles over, where something has caught her attention. "Marque' come over here and look at this." She holds up a box of condoms. "We need to get some of these super size condoms too, just in case Sweets wants to get it on again." Mae May teases.

"Yeah right! Sweety, after your last go around, don't count on it."

Mae grins, "Hater! You never know." Mae May puts a box in her basket and continues shopping. Marque' walks away.

"Mae May, look at these girl." Marque' says as he holds up a vibrator. "Here, put some of these regular sized vibrators in the basket as giveaways."

Mae May gets excited from her newly found treasure. "Marque' look at this chair." Mae May sits in the erotic looking chair that enhances sexual pleasures. "You can sit in it and have a ball all by yourself. Talk about a conversation piece. Now that would be a hit sitting next to the shampoo bowl." They laugh as they give each other a fist bump.

"Yes it would. Hell I'd never leave the area. In fact, I'd have to fire the shampoo girl if we put this in the salon." Mae May laughs, shaking her head in agreement with Marque' as they continue looking.

"Look at these," Marque' shows Mae May a display rack. "We have to get a few of these lingerie outfits to hang at the party for our erotic theme."

Mae May picks up one and begins displaying it against her body in a nearby mirror. "Hell, I want one of these sexy outfits to wear to the party."

"I need to get me one too," Marque' adds.

Suddenly Mae May starts feeling nauseated and holds her stomach. "I need to sit down. I don't feel good." They find a chair and Mae May sits down.

Marque' asks, "What's the matter?"

"I don't know. But the last time I felt like this I was pregnant."

Dumbfounded by the answer, Marque' responds. "Damn girl, not again! This will be baby number five!"

"Yeah tell me about it. I sure hope I'm not pregnant."

"I thought you were taking birth control pills?"

"I was, but they kept making me feel sick and gain weight so I stopped. I try to make sure the guy is using condoms, plus I use the rhythm method, or have him pull out before he comes if he doesn't have a condom."

"Isn't that how you came up pregnant the last three times? You know that shit don't work." Marque' sarcastically says.

"I don't wanna hear a damn lecture from you right now, especially with the way I feel!" She continues holding her stomach. She is rocking back and forth in the chair with her head leaning down. "Oh well, what's done is done. So, if you are pregnant who's this baby's daddy?"

With an evil look on her face, Mae May answers, "Hell, I don't know. This baby could be from several different guys, even Sweets."

Marque' raises his head in shock while being blown away with the realization. "Sweets' baby? Damn bitch now you're really messing it up for me by doing that shit. Besides, I thought he always uses condoms."

"He does. But remember, I told you that when me, him, and Cindy were getting our groove on, we got pretty wild and crazy, and it came off. Besides, we were so high that when we realized it came off, we said forget the condom, because he didn't have another one, and we kept screwing."

"Damn, damn, damn!" Marque' jumps up and down like a kid having a temper tantrum. "I sure hope Cindy was on some kind of birth control because Sweets has a lot of kids around town. His shit is potent! The girls he got pregnant tease him and say they got pregnant from him just looking at them too long, and winking his eyes at them."

Suddenly Mae May has a strange look on her face. "Well, then Cindy better watch out because she also wasn't taking anything since she hadn't been with a man in so long. She didn't think she needed any kind of birth control. Also, she knew Sweets was using a condom so she was cool, that is until his condom came off, then she kinda tripped. However, the sex was so good that she also got over it and said fuck it! We just kept doing our thang and having a ball!"

"Oh damnnnnnnnnnn!!! I sure hope she isn't pregnant too. If she is, both of you will be having, light skin, curly hair, brown eyed twins." he jokes.

"Let's not jump the gun. Hell, I haven't even taken a pregnancy test yet. So maybe I just ate something that didn't sit well with me."

Not Quite Good Enough

Marque' laughs out loud, "Yeah right bitch. Your problem is that you ate and screwed a large black joy stick without a condom and that isn't sitting well with you."

Mae May laughs, "Shut up bitch! You're just jealous, you hater."

"Damn right I'm jealous. Because of you bitches, Sweets may never deal with your asses again. Through you was gonna be the only way I could get to his cute ass. So yeah, I'm mad, jealous, AND a hater! Oh well, let me finish shopping for the party since we only have a week left. Hell, I've been in here so often, I practically know everything that's in here. So it won't take me long. You just sit here until you feel better. I can finish shopping alone."

"Ok, but before you leave can you get me a trash can? I think I'm gonna throw up." Marque' brings Mae May a trash can and right away she throws up. Marque' frowns at her, walks away, and continues picking out party favors and gadgets for the party.

T' La June

Twenty-Seven -*We're Pregnant*

While Tammy is finalizing her patients' files, Cindy asks, "Can you check me out before we leave? I haven't been feeling well lately. My stomach hurts. I've been feeling dizzy. The smell of certain things really make me sick. I hope I'm not coming down with the flu."

With a puzzled look on her face, Tammy responds. "You know, I haven't been feeling well either. I've been having some of those same symptoms. Where did we eat the last time?" Tammy asks Cindy while trying hard to remember and continues. "Maybe we ate something that made us sick. Let me check both of us out." Tammy checks Cindy's heartbeat with her stethoscope, looks into her eyes and mouth. "Here, go pee in this cup. Then I'll draw some blood and have it tested." Tammy gives Cindy the cup and she goes into the restroom. While Cindy goes to get her urine sample Tammy checks her own vitals and gets a pee sample in her private office restroom.

When Cindy returns with her cup, Tammy takes the cup and puts a pregnancy strip inside. Cindy looks at her strangely and asks, "Why are you checking for pregnancy? I just think I'm coming down with the flu. I've never been pregnant and haven't been with a man in awhile, so I can't be pregnant."

Tammy ignores her concerns and continues with the test and questions Cindy. "Well, it's easy to test for pregnancy, so I'll just check to rule it out for both of us. So, when did you have your last period?"

Cindy carefully thinks, "Umm, I can't remember. I normally start at the end of the month and now it's the middle of the next month. So yes, I am a little late. There's been so much going on lately that I hadn't paid attention." Cindy's thoughts go into full gear as she continues. "Now that I think about it, I am a few weeks late. Damn! I sure hope I'm not pregnant!" Cindy thinks back to her night of fun with Mae May, "Oh shit, could I be?"

Suddenly, while looking at the pee sample results from both of them Tammy yells, "Oh shit!"

"What?" Cindy questions.

With the strangest look on her face Tammy announces, "We're pregnant!"

Cindy laughs, "Girl, quit lying. Don't play like that. That shit ain't funny!"

Tammy takes another look at the test strips and say, "I'm not lying. The results of the urine test say we're both pregnant. Here, look at them." Tammy steps back so Cindy can see the results. They both look closely and in unison say, "Oh hell no!!!!"

"Tammy, come on now. You got to be kidding. I haven't been with anybody in almost a month."

Tammy lies, knowing she's had regular visits from Sweets for a few months and responds. "Me either."

Cindy says, "So whoever we were with last month is our babies' daddy!"

"Who were you with last?" Tammy asks Cindy an pries more. "Usually you tell me everything, but I can't remember you telling me anything about having sex. You only told me about the guy you met over the internet and I know you can't get pregnant over the internet." Tammy looks at her suspiciously while waiting for an answer.

Cindy covers up the truth, "Girl no! It was not my internet connection. Damn, it must be Ed's baby." Tammy looks at her with a shocked expression as Cindy continues. "Ed is an old boyfriend I dated in high school. He was my first love. I ran into him about a month ago while I was shopping. We ended up going out to dinner to catch up on old times. After dinner he took me home and we hooked up for a little sumthin-sumthin for old time sake. But that was it! I haven't seen him since because the sex was not good. In fact, it was so bad that it wasn't worth telling anyone about it. He wasn't worth the time of my day. That love connection will definitely not happen again! Hell, if you ask me, I would have preferred being at home knitting, rather than having sex with him, and I don't even knit." They laugh."

Even though Tammy is laughing, she's more than surprised by Cindy's confession. "How come you never told me about THAT hook up? I thought we were best-friends who tell each other everything?" Cindy smiles with embarrassment. "Yeah, I kinda kept that one to myself."

"Yeah you did, and you did it very well. But why?"

Cindy explains, "Tammy I knew you would have thought I was crazy or that Ed wasn't good enough for me because he's a custodian at the mall."

Tammy scolds Cindy, "Damn girl, you really lowered your morals with that one. What's up?"

Cindy smiles, "Yeah, I guess I did. But I was horny as hell and he was an old flame. He was the first guy I ever slept with. Besides, I hadn't screwed anybody in months. So, when I had an opportunity to get my groove on, that's what I did. I'm not proud of what I did. But yes, I had a weak moment and the damage is done now. So there, I said it! I'm not perfect and occasionally I get weak."

Tammy shakes her head in disappointment. "Well good for you. I'm glad you got your groove on for old time sakes. Although it looks like you're pregnant from your high school home-boy. I sure hope his custodian salary can take care of a baby. So now that you have his baby he'll end up sweet talking you into taking care of him too. But hey, you jumped into that bed, so now you'll have to lay in it."

Cindy shakes her head in disbelief and holds her hand toward Tammy face as to say, 'talk to the hand' and responds, "Whatever! But don't judge me now. What's done is done. So, since we know who my baby's daddy is, who's YOUR baby's daddy"? Cindy looks at Tammy with a smirk on her face.

"Chad." Tammy says while hiding the truth.

"Okkkk." Cindy reacts. "Since we know who our babies daddy's are, what are WE going to do?"

Tammy and Cindy react in an upset mood. Together they respond, "I don't know!" They begin crying and hugging each other.

Cindy holds her head down in disappointment and softly answers. "Tammy, I lied to you and I can't do that." Tammy looks at Cindy with a baffled look as she continues. "My baby's daddy isn't Ed."

From her tears Tammy asks, "Well who was it? Who's your baby's daddy?"

"Sweets."

"Sweets?" Tammy asks in amazement and confusion.

Cindy confesses. "Yeah, Sweets. I'm sorry I lied to you. I knew you really wouldn't approve of me being with Sweets, but you're my best friend. I can't lie to you about something so serious as this. So yes, me and Sweets had sex about a month ago. We got together when I went out with Mae May." Tammy shakes her head in disbelief as Cindy continues. "Damn! It must have happened when his condom came off. I knew I should have gotten up, but the sex was sooo damn good!" She stated shaking her head in denial.

"Sweets?" Tammy is still confused by her answer.

"Yes, Sweets." Cindy casually assumes.

Tammy begins playing back to herself the night when Sweets and her were together and his condom broke while they were having sex; her mind is in a daze.

"Tammy, did you hear me? You did say that Chad is the father of your baby, right?"

Tammy lies, "Yeah, it must be. Chad's the only person I've been with in awhile." Then she changes the subject to get the topic off of her. "But back to you pregnant by Sweets? That low-life, nonworking gigolo hoe? Cindy how could you stoop so low?"

Cindy feels worst from Tammy's comments. She holds her head down and silently cries as she explains. "I know what he does, but after hearing so much about how good in bed he is, I jumped at the opportunity." Suddenly Cindy's sad mood becomes those of guilt as she reminisces back to the moment. "I know what I did wasn't right. But at the time it didn't matter. All I could think about was if I didn't take the opportunity right then, I may never get the chance again. I figured I'd never know for myself if what everyone had said was true. Believe me, I was not disappointed one bit." Cindy smiles at the thought.

Tammy belittles Cindy as she responds, "Girl, you went wayyyyyyy down in the gutter for that. I sure hope it was good, because look at what happened because of your night of fun." Tammy turns her head in disgust and walks away.

Cindy defends herself and with confidence, stands up to Tammy for the first time. "Maybe I did go down to the gutter, but it's done now and I enjoyed the hell out of it. Besides, I couldn't tell you anything because I knew you would get mad and tell me what a low life he is. It was just one of those things that happened one night after we were partying and getting high."

"Getting high?" Tammy was totally blown away by her admission. "So now you get high and screw trash? Cindy, I don't know about you girl. This is wayyyy to much for me to handle right now." She shakes her head in disgust and begins to again walk away.

Cindy is angry and yells, "See, that's what I mean. You're always judging me. Yes, I got high and no I don't do it often. If I did, I'm a grown ass woman who can do what the hell she wants to do. But like I said, it was that one time. Me and Mae May have become good friends because you don't like to party. So we hang out a lot nowadays. I just don't tell you when we do because I don't want to

Not Quite Good Enough

here your criticism."

With a snotty attitude Tammy snaps back. "Well I've heard everything now. So help me get it right, it was you, Sweets, AND ghetto ass Mae May having an orgy? Is that what happened when you got pregnant?" Tammy puts her hand on her hip, leans back, and looks at Cindy with a judgmental expression.

Cindy smiles after realizing that what she did with Mae May and Sweets sounded crazy. "I guess I did, if you want to call it that. We just called it having fun."

In a sarcastic tone Tammy scolds, "Well, now your fun has gotten you pregnant. So what are you going to do now? Are you going to keep your baby or abort it? Because you know Sweets won't take care of you or your baby."

Feeling confident, Cindy stands her ground. "You're possibly right he won't take care of us, but I'm going to keep my baby. I will also take care of my baby alone if I have to." She becomes sympathetic and says, "Tammy, I'm 32 years old and have always wanted children but never had any. So I will keep my baby. I may never have any kids, and if this is my chance, then so be it. Hell, trying to find a good man may not ever come my way. If this is what it is, then I'll just have to accept the situation and deal with it. So what about you? Will you go back to Chad since he's the father of your baby?"

Tammy became angry, "Hell no! He ain't even working now. He can't do anything for me without a job. Hell, he can't even take care of himself let alone me and a baby. I for sure don't need that kind of drama just to have a daddy for my baby."

"So, will you keep yours? Will you raise your baby alone if you have too?" Cindy asks Tammy. "You also don't have any kids or a good man and you're 36. You know it's harder to get pregnant the older you get. It's a wonder we got pregnant now."

Tammy visualizes her sixteen year old daughter she had with

Sweets. She never told Cindy about her. Answering Tammy says, "You know, I'm going to have to think about it. I've always wanted to raise a baby. Maybe I will now that I'm older and financially secure. I don't know if I'll ever find Mr. Right. I seem to only find Mr. Right Now! Men just don't seem to be quite good enough for me." They laugh through their tears.

Cindy says sarcastically, "You can always turn to women. It's not such a bad thing, I've tried it."

Tammy laughs, "Hell no! I like dick too much. Did you like being with a woman?"

"Nahhh, it was just something I did one time with Mae May. That night with them was sooo awkward. I don't think I'll ever visit that path again."

"Thank God, because I don't want to have to be watching you from the back of my head. You might be checking out my butt." Tammy teases as they laugh.

"Girl, don't worry, you're good. I ain't looking at your ass, even though it's cute and round." Cindy jokes, causing Tammy to smirk and hide her behind with a patient's file.

"So tell me the story again about you and Sweets. I still can't believe you screwed him."

Cindy is more than willing to finally spill her guts about her one night stand. "Girl believe it. He was good as hellll! Sexually, he was everything every woman has ever said about him. I can see why women pay him. Brothas got it going onnnnn! I wanted to tell you so bad, but I just couldn't. I hope you understand and forgive me." Cindy has a happy, but puppy dog expression of sadness on her face. She goes to Tammy, hoping for a forgiveness hug.

Tammy smiles and hugs her back, "Girl please, I can't tell you how to run your life. I guess I have a bad habit of looking out for you. I only want the best for both of us. At the end of the day, you gotta do

Not Quite Good Enough

what you gotta do. But Sweets, damnnnn?" Tammy shakes her head smiling with Cindy smiling back. "All I have to say is you were really desperate!" they laugh as Tammy continues. "Although, you would think that a man who makes sex a part of his living would carry more than just one condom, the cheap bastard!" They chuckle again.

Cindy defends her pleasurable moment, "Don't knock it until you've tried it. At least my baby will be cute." She says trying to make light of the situation, then becomes serious. "Besides, why do you hate him so much?"

Tammy, making sure to not raise suspicion carefully answers, "I don't hate him. I just know how he uses women to get what he wants. He has a lot of babies running around town that need him and he doesn't even care for them. That pisses me off!"

Cindy is confused by her answer and said, "How do you know so much about him? And why do you even care?"

With her poker face on, Tammy regroups with her answer. "I only know what I hear. He got one of my friends pregnant years ago and then disappeared. Believe me, I don't care. But now you'll have to deal with the fact that he's your baby's daddy and your baby has a bunch of sisters and brothers running around town with no father to take care of them! But that's your decision. I just want you to be aware of what you're getting yourself into when it comes to Sweets, that's all." Tammy decides to change the subject. "Come on, let's drop the subject about Sweets and go home. We both have a lot to think about tonight. I sure hope we aren't having morning sickness tomorrow night at the party."

Cindy starts rubbing her stomach, "Yeah, me too. I guess this will take the fun out of us looking for a good man and getting our drink on."

"As for looking for a good man, not really. We still need a daddy for our babies. We don't want to look like two women who just sleep around with anybody and got pregnant. What we need to do is keep this information to ourselves in case we find Mr. Right at the party. Then we can say the baby is his and everyone can live happily ever after," Tammy admits.

"Damn girl, good thinking. I have to watch out for you. You have our entire problem solved with that plan." They laugh, close the doctor's office, and go home.

Not Quite Good Enough

Twenty-Eight - *The Big Party*

It's Valentine's Day. The night of the big party everyone has been waiting for. As a part of the party's theme, everyone ready to party is entering the hotel banquet room dressed in sexy lingerie. The room is decorated with a Valentine theme. Dangling from the ceiling throughout the room are red and white hearts, and cupid dolls with bows and arrows in their hands. The room is filled with red and white balloons, with formal table settings to match. There are several mannequins modeling sexy lingerie outfits in red, white, and black colors. Some of the dolls have sex toys and items in their hands such as whips, handcuffs, dildos, condoms, and more.

There are four half dressed, well built, bouncers standing at the door checking invitations. They are wearing only black bow ties around their neck, black long pants, and seductive smiles. Their shiny six pack chests are creating a warm smile on the faces of the many women and men as they enter. Marque', Mae May, and other salon owners are welcoming guests as they arrive. The owners and workers, of each salon, are dressed in revealing lingerie outfits, which captivate the arriving guests.

"Welcome to the *Sista Girls Salon and Barber Shop's* annual Valentine's Day party. Get your party favors over there." Marque' tells the guests as they come in. He shakes their hands while directing them to the table that displays mini key chains with naked penises, titty's, and butts as party favors.

"Heyyyy everybody, come on in. The party's right here." Mae May adds in her ghetto fabulous style like only she can.

Walking throughout the room are women servers wearing red sexy tight fitting babydoll lingerie. They are displaying an abundance of eye-catching cleavage.

On a nearby table as you walk into the room is a 'FREE Take

T' La June

One' sign. On that table is a large bowl of condoms and erotic party favors of all shapes and sizes. They are spread over the entire table. Positioned toward the back of the room is a large table full of soul food. Along the four corners of the room are bars complete with bartenders wearing black neck ties, black pants and smiles. They, too, are displaying shiny six pack chest muscles.

Amongst the guests are Vicki, Sophia, Kent, Tom, Brad, Aaron, Tommy, Billy, and Joe. They are talking in individual small groups.

"Look at these party favors. I see a few I want to take home." Sophia tells Vicki as she puts one of each in her purse.

"Me too, me too!" Vicki grabs with excitement as she continues to look and said, "See all those vibrators. They look very tempting. Man, if I knew they were going to have THESE kind of party favors, I would have brought my bigger purse; especially for that one over there." Vicki points to a large brown rubber penis and picks it up to observe. "Too bad we parked so far away. Otherwise, I'd take it to the car right now. I don't want to be walking around all night carrying a big ass vibrator. That would advertise I'm desperate, horny, and alone." Vicki holds up the large vibrator, makes sexual gestures while laughing.

"Well, we are, but I agree." Sophia adds and continues. "I wouldn't want to be seen with that in public either. That's for specially invited eyes only. Maybe it'll be here when we leave. I'm sure others would also be embarrassed to carry something that large around all night. Not many women bring large purses to parties. So, we'll check back before we leave. Then we can hide it under our jackets, long enough to get it out the door while going to our car. If not, we'll just have to pay a visit to the *Lotion & Motion Erotic Store*. Here," Sophia gives Vicki a business card. "Let's take one of their cards just in case we need to pay them a visit." They continue looking through the favors giggling like school girls while turning several power buttons on to high speeds to enjoy the demonstrations. After choosing the favors that could fit in their purses they walk over to the food table to mingle with guests.

"Look at all this food." Vicki admires the large selection. Displayed is: fried and baked chicken, catfish, waffles, greens, potatoes and gravy, mac & cheese, french fries, red beans & rice, corn, salad, rolls, sweet potato pie, peach cobbler, lemon and strawberry cake, bread pudding, chocolate cake, brownies, and cookies. "Umm, all my favorites, damnnnnnn! I'm lovin' being here. So much for my so-called diet tonight." Vicki begins filling her plate high.

"Same here," Sophia approves. She grabs two plates and begins filling them with everything. Then she looks across the room at the other guests and becomes disappointed. "Why did you have to invite Kent and Tom?"

"Because I wanted to. Why did you invite Brad?"

"Because he's my man now. We made it official last night that we're a couple. Then we had sex."

Vicki is surprised by the confession. She stops fixing her plate and says, "You had sex with him? Damn you bitch. You didn't tell me that one. So now you're keeping things from me I see." They hug and laugh as she continues, "That's good girl. I'm happy for you. Your ass finally got you some dick, AND a man, good for you. At least one of us is getting pleased sexually, because Kent can't satisfy me at all. You know the old saying, white men can't jump." Sophia shakes her head in agreement. "Well that's true in other areas too. But hell, those few moments under the sheets was what it was, just a few moments. You know it's been awhile since I've been with a man. I really needed to feel a real dick inside of me. I'm trying to remind myself what I've been missing. You know, sex without batteries and real skin. I'm also trying to decide if being with a man is really what I want, or am I just fooling myself."

"I hear you girl. If that's how you feel then why did you invite Kent especially since you're not really interested in him?"

"He overheard me talking on the phone about the party and invited himself. But it's cool. I don't have to spend the night with him. I can ditch him when I leave or tell him I'm sick if he tries to follow me home. I'll think of something. Unless I get horny from looking at all these half naked men. These ladies also look good in their sexy outfits." Vicki smiles as she checks out one of the women servers filling up a salad bowl. She is bending over exposing more cleavage while tossing the salad. "Ummm, she looks good. I think I want some salad." Vicki quietly says while licking her lips in lust.

"Did you say something?" Sophia asks.

Vicki quickly changes her thoughts, "I said, at least Kent is safe in case I need him for another screw." They laugh and continue filling their plates with Vicki keeping a close eye on the server.

Sophia adds, "Well, the way he's looking at you, I think he thinks you're gonna take him home with you tonight."

Vicki looks at Kent, frowns, and turns back to talk to Sophia. "Yeah I see that. Oh well, let him wish. I guess that isn't a crime." They laugh as she continues, "So tell me, if you and Brad are a couple, why didn't you bring him as your date?" Vicki questions.

"Because I knew you'd be alone and I promised to come with you. I'll hook up with him later. We don't want to rush things, or let too many people know we're a couple. We're taking things one day at a time."

Then a lady comes up to them smiling, "Hi Vicki. Long time no see."

Vicki begins blushing, but tries not to let it show. "Hi Stephanie. Yes, it has been a long time, in fact, too long." Vicki hugs Stephanie. "How are you?" Sophia noticing a love connection between the women begins to walk away to go to the restroom.

"I'll be right back." Sophia says with neither woman noticing her.

Not Quite Good Enough

The room is filled with hundreds of people who are dancing, mingling, and enjoying the sounds of the deejay. "Hey Billy, long time no see. How have you been?" Tommy, who was Marque's old boyfriend, says to Marque's current boyfriend.

"Good and you?" Billy says. He sarcastically thinks, "You sneaky ass tramp!"

"Good. I hear you and Marque' are living together now." Tommy asks pretending he doesn't already know.

Billy rolls his eyes thinking, "Like you didn't already know you bitch." Then he acts like the question was no big deal and becomes bubbly and happy. "Yeah, that's my man. We get along great! It's been fun living with him. So who are you dating now?"

"No one particular, just hanging with whoever right now. Ever since me and Marque' broke up I haven't found that special someone."

He sarcastically reminds Tommy, "Oh yeah, you guys broke up because you were screwing around on Marque'. I guess he wasn't good enough for you. We know that doesn't fly with him."

"Yes, I made a huge mistake, but we got past that and I apologized. We'll always be the best of friends." Tommy admits. He thinks, "Bitch, why you asking me some shit you already know. Umm huh, I'll be the last one laughing, just wait!"

Billy smiles and wonders, "I guess with you being here means you guys ARE still friends, but dammit, he's sleeping with me now. So eat your heart out bitch."

Uninterested in Tommy's conversation, Billy attempts to make Tommy feel bad by saying, "That's good because me and Marque' are doing great! We're having sooo much fun together. I certainly see what you saw in him because he's a good man, a one man's man. Too bad it didn't work out for you two. I'm sure you'll find that special someone soon."

Tommy frowns under his grin and admits, "Yes, I will. In fact, there's a few guys I'm checking out now. So, it's just a matter of time before I choose one that's right for me." He again thinks, "Bitch, you just don't know," then he smiles.

"I'm sure you will. Well, I gotta go and check on Marque'. I don't want him to miss me for too long. It's been nice seeing you again. Maybe we can all hang out one day soon."

"Yeah, maybe we can." Tommy said. But he was thinking, "Yeah right bitch! I wouldn't hang out with your ass if you were the last bitch on this earth."

"Well, gotta go get my man, talk to you later. Take care." Billy brags. Tommy thinks, "Bitch." Then blurts out loud. "Ok I will, and you too."

Billy slowly walks away smiling, knowing he pissed Tommy off with his conversation. Tommy watches him and smiles. He thinks, "You bitch. I'll keep taking care of your man since you don't seem to be enough man to handle all his needs. That's why he keeps coming to see me late at night when you're tucked away alone in your bed. He knows I know how to please all his needs." Tommy walks away to mingle with other guests.

Mae May and Marque' are still at the door welcoming guests when Sweets and his friends arrive. They are sharply dressed in suits. They walk in the room feeling confident and cocky; with their suave personalities and pretty boy looks. Mae May blushes as they come through the door but keeps quiet.

Sweets notices Mae May standing next to Marque' and smiles, licks his lips in a lustful way, walks over to her, and kisses her lips. "Damn baby, what you got on? You look good enough to eat." He talks softly in her ear as he admires her sexy and erotic lingerie.

Marque' smiles and whispers in Mae May's other ear after Sweets turns away saying, "You've done more than eat her already Sweet Daddy. Now it's my turn to eat you." Mae May smiles, nudges

Not Quite Good Enough

Marque' and gives him the evil eye to be quiet.

"Did you say something?" Sweets ask Marque'.

Marque' smiles, "No, I didn't say a word. Welcome to our party and come on in Sweet Daddy." He blushes and puckers his lips to kiss, at Sweets when his head is turned away.

Suddenly Mae May begins to feel bad. "Oh shit, I gotta throw up again." She runs to the restroom. Marque' shakes his head and continues welcoming guests.

"Hello ladies. Glad you could make it tonight." He acknowledges Tammy and Cindy as they walk in.

"Thank you." they say.

"Glad to be here." Tammy continues.

"Hey Marque', where's Mae May?" Cindy looks around the room in search of her.

"She hasn't been feeling well. She ran to the restroom." He smiles and points to the restroom.

Cindy is surprised by his answer. "Wow, me either. I better go see about her. Tammy, I'll be right back." Cindy goes to the restroom to check on Mae May. Meanwhile, Tammy walks around and admires the men in the room.

"Mae May are you in here?" Cindy says once she arrives at the restroom.

"Cindy is that you? I'm right here praying to the porcelain God." Throw up sounds are heard.

"Are you alright?" Cindy wets a paper towel with cold water.

"No, I feel like shit." Then you hear more throw up sounds.

Shortly after she tells Mae May, "Open the door, I have a cold towel for you." Mae May slowly reaches back, unlocks the door. Cindy comes into the stall and wipes her head. "Damn girl, you look like shit. What happened? What made you sick?" Mae May throws up again before she can answer. She makes so much noise that the echoing sounds of their voices can be heard outside the restroom door. Sweets is walking pass on his way to the men's restroom. The echo in the restroom is amplifying Mae May and Cindy's conversation in the quiet hallway. Sweets stops and listens to them talk.

Mae May throws up again. Cindy turns her head and walks away frowning. "Damn, I guess you don't feel good." Cindy says as she waits outside the stall for a few minutes.
"I'll be alright, just give me a few minutes."
"Ok but what's wrong? Why are you throwing up?" Cindy asks.
"I'm pregnant." Mae May confesses.
Cindy is surprised by the confession, "Pregnant? You too?"
Sweets overhears the conversation and begins to listen more closely.

Also surprised, Mae May looks up at Cindy and in a loud voice responds, "You're pregnant too? Oh shit!"

Cindy covers Mae May's mouth with a wet paper towel. "Shhhhh, not so loud. I don't want anybody to know right now."
"How do you know you're pregnant?"

"The last few weeks I haven't been feeling good. So I asked Tammy to check me out to see what was going on. I just thought I might have the flu or something like that. So when she told me I was pregnant I tripped out! Girl, I never thought I would get pregnant. Especially since I've never been pregnant before and I'm so old." Cindy admits.

"Well, since I've already been pregnant four times, when I started feeling bad I knew I was pregnant. I haven't even seen a doctor yet." Mae May confesses and then throws up again.

"Damn girl. You got this morning sickness bad. Doesn't your stomach know it's evening time?" Cindy laughs while turning her head away from Mae May. Mae May tries to laugh in-between her throwing up.

Cindy continues, "Well, there's nothing we can do now. What's

Not Quite Good Enough

done is done."

"Yeah, tell me about it." Mae May says while standing up to flush the toilet and wipe her mouth. "Now tell me how I'm gonna raise another baby, damn! Hell, it's hard enough raising four babies with just me and my mother. She's gonna be pissed at me when I tell her about baby number five. Damnnnn!" Mae May shakes her head in disbelief.

"Well, if it'll make you feel any better, Miss Prissy, as you call her, Tammy, is also pregnant." Cindy admits. "But don't tell her I told you."

While washing her face Mae May looks up from the sink dumbfounded and says, "Damnnnn, Tammy too? Cindy, you gotta be lying. Come on girl, don't lie to me like that. I can't believe that shit. April Fool's day isn't here yet. So quit tripping and tell me the truth."

Cindy starts laughing as she responds. "Girl, I am telling you the truth. I wouldn't lie about something like that!"

Mae May again shakes her head in disbelief, "Damn girl, this is a trip. All three of us pregnant at the same time? I can't believe this shit! This is a damn shame."

"Yes it is, so who has little miss good girl been screwing? One of those rich white guys?"

"Yeah, a guy named Chad who she's been screwing off and on for awhile."

"Wow, I still can't believe this shit." Mae May gets up and flushes the toilet again. "I think me and you got pregnant from Sweets when we were all together and his condom came off. What you think?" Cindy shakes her head to agree as Mae May continues, "Because all the other brothas I've been with had no problem with their rubbers. You said you haven't slept with anyone in months. So it has to be Sweets."

Cindy agrees again, "Yeah, I think you're right because he's the only guy I've been with in months. He's definitely my baby's daddy."

"Yeah, I believe he's mine too because I had quit taking my pills. They were making me sick and gain weight. I figured I'd be good as long as the guy was using a condom." Mae May says.

After hearing the confessions from the girls, Sweets almost chokes but remains quiet to hear the rest of the conversation.

"Damnnnn, our babies will be sisters. Now that's a trip," Mae May says, then runs back to the stall and throws up again. Cindy shakes her head and waits at the sink for her to be done.

After Mae May finishes, she goes to wash her hands and face. "You said Tammy is pregnant by some rich white guy named Chad? It's a wonder her prissy ass got pregnant at all, especially since she's a big time doctor who thinks she knows so damn much. She can tell everybody else how to live their life, and now SHE'S pregnant, ain't that a trip!"

"Yeah tell me about it. Chad used to be rich but he recently lost his job and everything he owned. He was investing in the stock market when everything crashed. Now she doesn't want him anymore."

"Figures, the greedy bitch." Mae May said. "Well, I don't have time to worry about her when my ass can't stop praying to the porcelain God! Hell, I have my own damn problems." They laugh as Mae May throws up again.

"I heard that. Thank God I haven't gotten as sick as you, I sure hope I don't. Right now the only thing I feel is a little nauseated in the morning. After I throw up and eat I feel better. But damn girl, if you don't stop throwing up you won't be able to enjoy the party."

"I'll be alright, I just need to stay in here a little while longer."

"Are you sure?"

"Yeah, I'll be alright. I'm starting to feel better now that I got

Not Quite Good Enough

everything out of my system that I ate today. But if I eat the food tonight my black ass will be right back in here. I think I'll be fasting for the rest of the night." Mae May laughs. She gets up, flushes the toilet again, and washes her face and hands.

Marque' walks up and notices Sweets eavesdropping. "Hey Sweets, what's up? Is there something I need to hear too? Because you know I love good gossip." Marque' said as he also tries to listen.

Sweets quickly moves away from the door and acts like he's going to the men's restroom. "Hey Marque', I wasn't listening to anything. I just had a bad reception on my phone and it seems to work better over here. Excuse me man, I gotta handle my business." Sweets walks away and goes into the men's restroom. Marque' is puzzled by Sweets' reaction. All of a sudden Mae May and Cindy walk out of the ladies restroom laughing.

"Hey ladies." Marque' said as they walk out. "I sure hope you weren't talking about anything private in there."
Mae May is surprised by his comment, "Why?"
"Because Sweets was standing at the door eavesdropping."

Mae May and Cindy look at each other with shocked expressions and in unison say, "Oh Shit!"

Mae May looks at Cindy and Marque' and says, "Well, if he heard anything he wasn't suppose to hear, he would have found out eventually. So, what the hell. I'm not gonna worry about it. He ain't gonna do anything about it anyway, so why trip."

Cindy is worried, "I hope he didn't hear everything. I don't want Tammy to get mad at me for telling her business."

Mae May explodes, "Girl, forget about what Tammy thinks, the skinny ass bitch. You're always trying to please her ass. Hell, you better start thinking about yourself and quit thinking about her all the goddamn time. Cindy, you're a grown ass woman who can do and say what the hell she wants' to say. So fuck her!"

Marque' looks surprised by what's actually going on. "Well, whatever he heard, he heard. It's too late to take it back. Now, I gotta pee, I'll see you guys on the dance floor. And Mae May, don't throw up on the dance floor because if you do, I'm bringing your black ass the mop bitch," he smiles and walks away.

They laugh as Mae May argues back, "You mean to tell me that you wouldn't clean up my mess?"

Marque' turns around as he's entering through the restroom door, "Hell no!" He then goes into the men's restroom.

As Mae May and Cindy begin to return to the party, they notice Sophia and Brad sneaking pass them. The two are heading toward the women's restroom, giggling like school kids. They were walking so fast, they never noticed Mae May and Cindy passing them. They're constantly looking around to see if anyone's coming their way before disappearing into the closed restroom door. Once Sophia and Brad are out of site, Mae May and Cindy tip-top back to the restroom, open the door, and quietly peek in. The room is quiet and empty, when suddenly bumping and moaning sounds are quietly heard from behind a closed stall. "Ohhhhh, ohhh, ahhhhh! Oh baby, you feel sooo good! Yes, yes, yessss!" Were the sounds of a females voice. Mae May and Cindy quietly giggle and tip-toe out the door.

Once outside the restroom, Mae May whispers, "Sounds like there's gonna be another baby coming into this world real soon." Cindy smiles and agrees as the two rejoin the rest of the party people in the main room. Soon after, Cindy joins Tammy while Mae May returns to the front entrance of the party to greet clients and friends.

"Damn girl, what took you so long? Did you fall in the toilet or something?" Tammy asks.

Cindy answers with a whisper. "Mae May was throwing up because she's pregnant. But don't tell her I told you." Cindy looks around the room to make sure Mae May isn't standing near her.

Not Quite Good Enough

In a whisper, Tammy asks, "Did you tell her you are too?"

"Yeah." Cindy quietly answers.

"I hope you didn't tell her I was too." Tammy immediately responds.

Cindy covers her tracks by lying, "Oh nooo, I didn't tell her your business." She answers with a straight, but guilty look. She quickly changes the subject and begins to walk toward the food table. "Let's get something to eat. Are there a lot of cute guys here that aren't gay?"

Tammy becomes curious at Cindy's behavior, but follows. "Yes, there seems to be several." Once at the food table, Sweets approaches.

"Hello ladies. You look nice tonight." Sweets replies with a laid back tone. He winks his eye at each of them. Tammy acts like she didn't hear him and fixes her plate. Sweets looks at her, shaking his head negatively. He begins aiming his attention toward Cindy.

Cindy admires the attention and smiles when she visualizes their time together, "Thank you."

"Well, I just wanted to say hi. I gotta get back to my boyz over there. I'll check you ladies out later," Sweets said as he looks at Tammy with a displeased expression and walks away. Tammy is still ignoring him.

Cindy is blown away with Tammy's rudeness, "How come you're so rude to him? He didn't do anything to you. He's actually a nice guy if you get to know him."

"That's YOUR baby's daddy, not mine!" Tammy whispers with an aggressively bad attitude. "I don't have to ever talk to him. In fact, he isn't worth my time at all. Just prepare your plate and quit asking so many questions. You know I don't like Sweets, nothing else needs to be said, period." Tammy continues compiling her plate, while a disappointed Cindy tries to ignore her comments. Cindy fills her mouth with food so she wouldn't be tempted to say something she'd regret.

On the other side of the room we see Vicki and Stephanie in deep conversation. "So are you seeing anyone now?" Vicki asks. Stephanie displays disappointment and says, "Not since me and you broke up last year."

Vickie immediately feels hopeful. "Okkkk," she said with a smile on her face. "So, what brings you here, especially since you knew I'd be here and you don't want me anymore?"

"You." Stephanie boldly responds with confidence. "Yes, I knew you would be here, that's why I came. Marque' did my hair last week and told me you'd be here. He said he also did your hair and makeup and that you were looking like a new person. He was right, you look really nice." Stephanie craves for Vickie with sex and lust in her eyes.

Vicki tries to act uninterested, "Thank you, you do too."

"Vicki, I also came to tell you that I miss you and want you back in my life. Will you take me back?"

Vicki's uninterested mood suddenly changes to happiness as she smiles, "You do?"

"Yes, I do!" Stephanie says with affection.

Vicki confesses, "Stephanie, I miss you too! To tell the truth, my life hasn't been the same since you left me. After you left I never thought I was quite good enough for anyone. I've been lost without you. I didn't know which direction my life would go once you broke up with me."

The words coming out of Vicki's mouth is brightening up the entire room for Stephanie. "I felt the same way too. Please forgive me, I was confused! I thought I wanted to be in a relationship with a man. Now I know what I want, and all I want is you!" Then Stephanie hesitates, "That is if you'll have me back."

Vicki begins blushing, "All you're saying are just a few words,

Not Quite Good Enough

I'm back baby!" They hug and tears of joy begin falling. She continues, "After the dance lets go to my place and make love because I've missed you a hell of a lot."

Stephanie blushes and jokes and mimics Vicki's line, "All you're saying are just a few words. I'm here for only you!" Stephanie and Vicki passionately kiss right in the middle of the crowded room afterwards. They walk toward the food and fix a plate to eat. They are holding hands, smiling, and looking into each other's eyes with gleam.

With pain, love, and laughter in the air, Marque' notices tension as Billy walks away from Tommy. He stops him and said, "Is everything alright?"

"Yes, everything's just fine." Billy says with a snappy tone. He kisses Marque' and looks at Tommy to see if he's looking.

"I saw you talking to Tommy, are you guys cool?"

"Yes, I said everything's just fine." Billy admits.

"Good, I want to say hi to him." Marque' says as he begins to walk toward Tommy. Billy just stands there, "Come with me."

Billy hesitantly comes with Marque' while attempting to act like everything is alright. Billy knows the loving, yet lustful past Marque' shared with Tommy. However, he didn't realize the present situation they share.

The uneasy vibes Marque' is feeling from Billy did not reveal what he was walking into. "Billy, are you alright?"

"Yes, I'm fine." They continue walking toward Tommy.

Beaming light a star, Tommy greets Marque', "Hey Marque'," he says while acknowledges him with a flirtatious tone. "How you doin'?" Tommy says with both hands bent downward under his face, slatting his eyes, and bottom lip down.

Billy becomes angry at the flirtatious expressions on Tommy's face and sarcastically responds, "He's doing just fine. I see to that every night. Thank you very much." Billy hugs Marque', turns his face toward him, and passionately tongue kisses him.

Marque' knows that Billy is trying to make Tommy jealous, he pulls away and smiles. "Come on guys, lighten up. I'm all about making love, not war. There's enough of my love to go around for everyone." Billy has a cynical look on his face. Marque' reassures his commitment, "Billy, I'm with you now, so you don't have to trip with Tommy. Tommy, our thang was in the past but we can all be friends now, can't we?" Marque' looks at both of them, waiting for a response.

Tommy frowns at the notion and fires back, "That's not what you were saying last night when we were together in the back seat of your car while at the club, orrrr, the week before when we made love in the club's restroom stalls."

Billy immediately gets defensive and reaches for Tommy to hit him. Marque' stops his swing and becomes angry. "Hey, we're not gonna have any of that here. Calm down! Billy, you're my man now and that's the only thing that matters." Tommy smiles as Marque' gives him an evil look.

Billy snatches away from Marque' and gives him a furious look as he expresses himself, "Marque', I thought I was your man. What you doing screwing him?"

Tommy is all smiles as he fires in defense of Marque', "Shut up bitch. You're just not man enough for him and you never were. He only wants you for your money. But he comes to me to be pleased." Billy swings again to hit Tommy, but Marque' again blocks his swing.

"Look, don't embarrass me!" Marque' angrily fires back, "I'm not going to stand for all this shit tonight or any night. Billy, I love you and that's all you need to know. Tommy, it's over between us. All we can ever be is friends. So, if you can't treat my man with respect, you can leave. I am not going to have you guys fighting over me. Hell,

Not Quite Good Enough

we spent too much damn money on this event to make it successful. We don't need you two to mess it up. So, either you guys get along, or someone is leaving. Now, you know it ain't gonna be me. So what's it gonna be?" Marque' gives both of them the evil eye as he waits for a response.

"I'm cool." Billy responds with a smile of defeat on his face.

Tommy reacts, "I'm cool too." He turns his head away looking angry.

"Good, because I love both of you." Marque' utters. "But Tommy, I want you to understand that Billy and I are a couple now and that's not going to change anytime soon." Marque' takes Billy's hand and said, "Come on Billy, I want to introduce you to someone. I'll talk to you later Tommy." Marque' and Billy walk away. While Marque' is looking, Billy is waving and smiling at Tommy with a conquering gesture. However, once Marque's back is turned, Billy turns his head around and sticks his tongue out at Tommy. Tommy then gives him a 'fuck you' finger gesture. Tommy is left standing alone, embarrassed and fuming with anger.

At the dessert table Tammy, Cindy, and Mae May are tasting and choosing desserts to eat. "Umm, this sweet potato pie is good." Mae May takes a bite of pie she has put on her plate.

Cindy follows, "It sure is." She then encourages Tammy to try a bite. "Here, taste it." Cindy offers her a taste of her slice.

Tammy frowns and turns her head in the opposite direction, then whispers in Cindy's ear. "After what you told me about you, Sweets, and Mae May, I don't ever want to eat after you." Tammy jokes and continues with a more serious, louder tone. "But for real, I don't want any. The smell is making me sick."

Mae May teases, "Is there a baby brewing in your pot too?"

Tammy becomes defensive. "Hell no, who told you that shit?" She immediately looks at Cindy, as Cindy turns her head in the opposite direction.

Mae May laughs, "Damn girl, lighten up. Nobody told me anything. I was just joking with you." She winks her eye at Cindy.

Suddenly Sweets approaches the table with his three friends and they fix a plate with some dessert. Mae May and Cindy get nervous.

"What's going on lovely ladies?" Sweets asks the three.

With a nervous tone, Mae May answers. "Hi Sweets. Are you enjoying the party?"

"Yes I am." He smiles as he looks around the room. "In fact, I'm enjoying more than the party, I'm enjoying all these beautiful ladies here tonight. Lord have mercy! Mo' money, mo' money, moooo money!" He brags while looking around the room searching for more ladies. Tammy is frowning so Sweets addresses her personally. "Tammy, why you always giving a brotha such a hard time? I didn't do anything to you."

Tammy rolls her eyes at him and answers angrily, "Don't talk to me. I don't have time for your bullshit." She attempts to walk away when Sweets continues his conversation to her in a loud and aggressive tone.

"Bitch, I thought we talked about you fronting me off a few days ago." Tammy stops to prevent him from getting louder. Mae May and Cindy are standing in amazement with their mouths wide open as they listen to Sweets embarrass Tammy.

With an air of arrogance and a whispered tone, Tammy gets right in his face and tries to save herself from embarrassment before it's too late. "I haven't talked to you about anything, nor have I wasted my precious time with the likes of you. So what are you talking about?" Tammy begins to sweat as people start to gather closer.

In a loud tone, Sweets continues, "Well, you had time for me the other night when we made love at your condo, in your big fluffy bed with the white lace sheets. In fact, I like the new white bedspread you have now, because the pink one you had last month was a little too gay for me." Everyone around them looks surprised and chuckles. He continues, "So, why don't you have time for me now? You think you're too good for me? Is that what it is? Because the money you paid me bought me this pretty new suit I have on. Everyone knows Sweets doesn't buy cheap." He strikes a pose, turns in a complete circle to show off his suit. He waits for an answer. The crowd makes comments under their breath. This attracts more people; causing them to hang on to his every word.

    Mae May and Cindy are stunned with the conversation. Sweets is smiling and eating a piece of pie. Tammy stands there embarrassed. His friends and others are smiling while looking at Tammy, who is turning red.

    Suddenly a lady from the crowd adds her two cents, "I still have time for you Sweets. Come home with me tonight, I'll pay you, and let you satisfy my sexual needs."

    A second woman also responds, "Yeah Sweets, you can come visit me once you're done with her. I got some money for you too. Then you can buy yourself another suit." Everyone laughs as tears begin to fall from Tammy's eyes, as she is frozen in time.

    Angry, Mae May looks at Tammy and shakes her head in disbelief and she adds to the comments, "Damn girl, I didn't know you rolled like that, and with Sweets, too? He's the main person you're always downing and telling Cindy she shouldn't give the time of her day to. Yet you're giving up more than time. You're giving up money and ass. I knew you were a lying ass bitch, but damnnnn, I didn't know you were sleeping with the so-called enemy." Mae May looks at Cindy, who also has tears in her eyes. "See Cindy, I told you not to listen to her. This bitch is always going around saying who's not good enough for someone when all along, all she wanted was a juicy joy stick like the rest of us!"

T' La June

Angry and embarrassed, Tammy finally fires back strong, "Fuck you Mae May and you too Sweets. I don't have time for all this bullshit, I'm out of here." Tammy begins pushing herself away from the crowd to head toward the door.

Cindy is puzzled and disappointed but adds to the conversation, "Oh, so you can dish shit out, but you can't take shit? Just like a bitch!" She says to Tammy, then looks around the room and focuses her conversation directly at Sweets. "Sweets, did I mention that Tammy is pregnant? And from what you just told us, you might be her baby's daddy." The whole room gasps.

Tammy looks at Cindy with fire in her eyes. "You can't talk because both of you bitches are also pregnant with his child." Tammy points to Cindy and Mae May as the crowd is even more surprised. The clatter of talk within the room is waiting for the next blow of words.

Sweets is surprised by the comment and jokingly shakes his head in amazement. Then whispers loud enough for many to hear, "Damn, I knew I should have bought better condoms." They laugh as he continues. "Well, I love all my kids, at least the ones I know about." he jokes. Then, with a serious look he walks over to Tammy and looks directly into her eyes. "By the way Tammy, I still want to meet the daughter we had together in high school. You know, our sixteen year old daughter Danielle." Everyone's mouth opens wide in disbelief as the whispers again flow. The music suddenly stops playing while everyone carefully listens in.

Cindy is more angry by what she just heard. "Oh hellll no! Sweets, what did you just say?"

"I said your goody-two-shoes girl Tammy already has my baby. In fact our baby, whom I have yet to meet, is a high school senior. Isn't that right Tammy?" He gives her a sarcastic look.

Tammy is crying. "Fuck you Sweets! Or should I say, fuck

Not Quite Good Enough

you Frank Jones for those of you looking for him." Sweets is furious with Tammy's comments, and gets into her face. He pulls his hand back as though he's going to slap her, but instead turns around and walks away.

    Cindy continues, "You mean to tell me that you already have a baby by Sweets? You never told me that. Hell, you never told me you even had a baby, and I'm supposed to be your best friend. You had me thinking that this was the first time you got pregnant. Then you told me that the baby was by a white man. Tammy, you're a skinny, prissy ass bitch, who thinks that you're better than everybody else. You're no better than the rest of us. You had me thinking I was too good for anyone, including a brotha with a low paying job that works hard." She looks over at Joe who's standing quietly, smiling, and shaking his head to agree with her statement. Cindy continues, "That's why I couldn't get a man. I never thought anybody was good enough for me. But now I hear your real story. You're a real stuck up, fake ass bitch!"

    Tammy slaps Cindy in her face. "Shut up bitch, I don't tell you everything! Even if I did I would have never told you about my daughter. She isn't any of your business, or anyone else's business in this damn town. Cindy, as far as you getting a man, you still couldn't get one even if you tried because you're a phoney bitch, not me. You're always trying to be somebody you aren't. You're always trying to live like you're rich, when you're not. All you want in a man is his money, not a man who will love you. A good man can see right through that shit. So don't blame your problems on me. Take responsibility for your own damn self." Mae May grabs Cindy's hand and holds it back from slapping Tammy.

    With a furious look in her eye, Mae May glares at Tammy, while talking to Cindy and says, "Cindy, she isn't worth you hitting her since she's your so-called best friend and boss. But I'm not." Mae

May then slaps Tammy so hard her face turns red, he lip begins to bleed, and Tammy almost falls to the floor. The crowd roars with excitement as Cindy pulls Mae May away from hitting Tammy again. Mae May wipes the blood off her hand and continues. "Don't worry, I'm not gonna hit her again. Because if I do, I might kill the skinny bitch. But Tammy, don't ever mess with my friend again, or your ass will be mine! I promise you that!" The crowd is still roaring with chatter. Mae May then looks at Tammy and sarcastically says, "Now, your mouth matches the colors of our Valentine's Day party."

"No Mae May, leave her alone. She isn't worth it." Cindy says as Mae May steps back.

"I'm done." Mae May says.

Tammy wipes the blood off her mouth and rages with words. "Mae May you bitch! Your ass will see me in court, I promise you that!"

Cindy then fires back, "Tammy, that's what you get. You can't talk bout me not being able to get a good man, because you can't get one your own damn self. You're always telling everybody else how to live their lives, when you don't know how to live your own life." Cindy steps away and holds her hands high in the air, signaling she's done fighting and continues, "It's all good, I'm cool now. My baby and I will be just fine. I guess now our kids will be related. So what you think of that?"

Suddenly Sweets joins in, "Oh hell no! Hold up all you bitches. Sweets is a lover man. I don't have time to be nobody's daddy. So you bitches are gonna have to work that shit out on your own. It ain't like you can garnish my wages to get any money." he jokes. "I don't do business with the IRS. I only do business with my bitches!" He mocks.

One of the ladies from the crowd yells, "Sweets, I'm right here for ya suga!"

Not Quite Good Enough

Mae May looks at the lady and reacts, "Shut up you stupid bitch. We're talking some real business here." Everyone laughs as she continues. "Sweets, your ass is definitely gonna take care of me and my baby, so I don't know what you're talking about."
Cindy joins in, "Yeah, mine too."

"Yeah right, ya'll's ass's better go file papers at the local welfare office because that's the only support you'll be getting," Sweets threatens. "Cindy, after blasting on Tammy the way you did, you better also file papers at the unemployment office. I'm sure that you don't have a job anymore with all that bullshit you were saying. And Mae May, getting support for another baby won't be hard for you at all. Especially since you already have a mile long file, at the welfare office, from all the other disowned babies you got. All of you bitches can kiss my pretty black ass!" He grabs his dick and pulls up, gesturing fuck you.

At that moment, Mae May throws up on Sweets' shiny black shoes and black designer suit. Everyone laughs as he yells, "You damn bitch, dammit, all on my brand new suit. Your ass is going to buy me another suit."

Mae May wipes her mouth on his jacket as he pulls it away from her and she laughs, "Get the damn welfare office to buy you a new suit because your black ass ain't getting a goddamn penny from me, and I mean that shit!"

Marque' breaks up the fight, "Ok ladies, that's enough. This has gone on far too long. Everyone, go back to the party. Sweets, it's time for you to leave. Mae May, Tammy and Cindy, you bitches need to talk this shit out. Don't let no man, who won't even stand up as a man, break up your friendships. Go sit your asses down and work this shit out now." He points to each of them, directing them to leave the area.

With her makeup running down her face, Tammy yells in

anger, "Cindy, you're fired. Don't say another word to me ever again." Embarrassed, Tammy then yells, "I've gotta get out of here now." Tammy begins running toward the door.

A man from the crowd yells, "Wait Tammy, let me walk you to your car." Tammy storms out the room with the mystery man following. Marque' goes to the microphone and gets the party going again.

Mae May and Cindy go to a table and sit down to talk. "Can you believe the shit that just happened?" Mae May asks. "I knew that bitch had some skeletons in her closet, but I didn't think they were that damn bad! But girl, I'm sorry you lost your job. Don't worry, you'll find another one." Mae May and Cindy hug each other as Cindy cries.

Then Cindy looks at Mae May and smiles, "Girl, I'm not worried about that shit now. But don't be too hard on her. I'm sure she did what she felt she had to do. I ain't mad at her. I would have done the same thing. Give her a little time to cool off; she'll be alright."

"But she fired you."

"Mae May, I've been around Tammy for a long time and I know her as if she was my sister. Everybody's got some skeletons in their closets. Trust me, she'll be okay in a few days. She just said all that shit so she wouldn't be too embarrassed. She ain't that cold. She just needs time to chill. Besides, the guy following her is Chad, the guy I told you she was dating off and on. That white boy loves the panties off her black ass. Maybe after what happened tonight she'll realize that he is good enough for her after all. At least she won't have to raise her baby alone like we will."

Suddenly a man comes to their table, "Excuse me ladies." Cindy and Mae May look at the good looking guy and smile. "Yes" they say together.

The handsome man is directing his conversation toward Cindy.

Not Quite Good Enough

"I couldn't help but over hear the conversation. May I reintroduce myself to you?" he says smiling.

Mae May is looking puzzled as Cindy smiles.

"Yes you may." Cindy responds with a smile as she remembers their first meeting, in the restaurant parking lot. She was reminded of who he was when she and Tammy talked down to him for being just a sales assistant.

"My name is Joe. I've been watching you all night. But I didn't have the nerve to talk to you after what happened when we first met. I knew you wouldn't talk to a plain guy like me. So if what I heard is true, I'd like to know if I can talk to you now? You see, I'm looking for a good woman and I don't have a problem taking care of you or raising your baby."

Cindy and Mae May look at each other, then look at him as Mae May blushes, "Damn, I guess some good did come out of all this crazy shit. Do you have any friends here tonight for me? I'm also looking for a daddy for my soon-to-be baby and my other four babies at home."

Joe laughs, "I'm not sure if my boyz can handle five babies, but I know I can sure handle one." He looks deep into Cindy's eyes and continues. "I've always wanted a baby and at 38 years old I'm not so sure if that'll ever happen. So, what do you say, can we talk and get to know each other a little better?"

Cindy begins blushing, "I would love to talk to a real man."

He holds out his hand for her to take and said, "Well, let's go sit down at another table and get to know each other a little better." Cindy gestures yes as he helps her get out of her chair and points to an empty table for them to sit.

Mae May looks at them and smiles as they walk across the room. She says to herself, "Well excuse the hell out of me. I'll just keep looking. I guess everybody ain't good enough!"

T' La June

  Cindy and Joe find a seat and enjoy their conversation. Mae May walks away happy for her friend.

  As the night moves on and the party ends, several people are leaving as a couple. Sophia is with Brad, Vicki is with Stephanie, Marque' is with Billy, and Cindy is with Joe, while Mae May leaves alone, still feeling sick.

  "Wait," Vicki says as her and Stephanie get ready to walk out the door. "I forgot something." Stephanie is puzzled as Vicki runs back to the table to grab the large penis she wanted when she arrived. Stephanie laughs as Vicki comes back smiling. Vicki kisses Stephanie and says, "We're gonna need this tonight." They then hug and walk out the door.

Not Quite Good Enough

Twenty-Nine - *One Year Later*

It's one year later when Tammy, Cindy, and Mae May meet up at a local park with their babies. The day is sunny and warm as they come together feeling happy. Once together, they give each other a group hug.

"Hey girls, How you doin'?" Mae May asks, while displaying the hand gesture and facial expressions dubbed from the famous Wendy greeting, as everyone sits down on a cement bench.

Cindy smiles and replies, "Good. So 'How YOU doin'?'"

Mae May and Tammy grin. Tammy then adds, "Everything's good with me too."

"I'm good too, just busy." Mae May echoes. "I've been so busy with the kids that I hardly have time for myself. Once I got pregnant with Re-Re I decided to settle my fast ass down. I decided it was time for me to be a full time mother to my babies rather than a part time mother." The ladies nod their heads in agreement as Mae May continues. "Besides, they need their mother. Hell, they were at the point where they would call for my mother when they wanted something when I would also be in the same room. They wouldn't even want me to help them. At first I didn't care, as long as I could party. After awhile that shit started to really bother me, so I had to stop it. Hell, I'm the momma, not MY momma!" Mae May grins and carries on. "For the first time they're calling me Momma and not Mae May. Besides, my ass is getting too old for all that partying. I can't hang like I used too. I also tied my tubes so I won't get pregnant again."

"It's about damn time." Cindy says as her and Tammy nod in agreement.

Mae May laughs, "That's cold ya'll, but that's alright. Enough is enough. After having five babies with five different daddies that sure is enough! So I'm through having babies!" They smile while agreeing.

"Girl, I heard that," Tammy adds. "Chad and I got married before I had the twins so he could adopt them. I wanted them to have a real and official daddy before they were born. I wanted someone who would love them as much as I do, you know an unconditional kind of love. When I had them, Chad was even in the delivery room with me. He held my hand the entire time. He kept me as calm as could be considering the circumstances. Then my beautiful babies were born." Tammy calmly says.

Suddenly Cindy interrupts by loudly clearing her throat, looks dead at Tammy, and with an excited high-pitched tone says, "Excuse me?" Cindy is making sarcastic facial expressions. Tammy has a puzzled look on her face as Cindy continues. "Aren't you forgetting to mention the part about when all hell broke loose!"

Mae May looks at Cindy and then at Tammy, trying to figure out what Cindy's talking about and says, "What are you talking about? What do you mean, when all hell broke loose? What happened?" Cindy points out, "Did you see Tammy's twins?"

Mae May goes to the double seated stroller, lifts up the blanket and get the surprise of her life. "What the hell happened here? Who's babies are these? I thought you said you had twins? These babies do NOT look like twins." Mae May waits for Tammy to answer.

"I did have twins. These are my babies." Tammy grins.

Mae May throws up one hand, places the other over her mouth, and responds, "Wait just a damn minute, let me get this correct. One baby has brown skin with brown eyes and black hair, and the other one has white skin with blond hair and blue eyes. Ok, so what the hell happened? Because you and Sweets couldn't have made a black AND a white baby! Come on Missy, if both of these babies are yours, you got some damn explaining to do."

Cindy begins laughing so hard she has tears falling from her face.

Tammy also laughs and then explains. "That was the exact reaction Chad and I felt when the babies came out. Chad looked at me and I looked at him, we knew something wasn't right. So, I had to confess to everyone in the delivery room that I had slept with both Chad and Sweets within days of each other. Once I confessed, my doctor told me that I may have conceived from both men. So he took a DNA test and proved that my twins are a one in a million rarity. He said it has happened before."

Mae May is blown away and wants more details. "Damn girl, tell me more. How did this shit happen? Is it possible that a woman can have a baby by two different men? I thought that kinda shit only happens with dogs. You for damn sure ain't a dog, or are you one in disguise?" They laugh.

Tammy, shakes her head with laughter, then looks at Mae May and responds, "I'm afraid it is possible. Since I'm a doctor, I've heard of this kind of thing happening when I was in medical school. I just never thought I'd live to meet anyone in this situation, until it happened to me. Then I also remember seeing it on TV when it happened to a couple and thought how crazy of a story it was. Now, the story is mine." In a serious tone, Tammy then explains her theory as a medical professional would explain. "You see, normally every month a woman's ovary releases one egg that can be fertilized by one sperm. However, in my case, a pair of eggs were released. During the time when I slept with Chad one day and Sweets the next day, my body had allowed two of my eggs to become fertilized. Since a sperm can remain alive and well for up to five days in the reproductive tract, it allowed both of my eggs to generate a fetus. Therefore, as in my case, because I had sex with two different men within that five day period, it allowed each person's sperm to wait for an egg to be released and then fertilized."

Mae May is in disbelief as she listens to Tammy talk doctor talk. "Excuse me, but can you explain this shit to me like I'm a fifth grader, because this shit is wayy crazy over my head!" Mae May says.

Tammy and Cindy laugh as Tammy continues to explain. "Ok, here's the version as it you are a fifth grader, I slept with Sweets one day, a few days later, I slept with Chad. Then, two of my eggs were released, and each mans sperm was still in me and they each fertilized one of the eggs. My babies are fraternal twins, it's just that they have two daddies."

"Damnnnnnnnnnnnn." Mae May says as she shakes her head in disbelief. "Now, THAT'S a trip!" Mae May acknowledges.

Tammy continues. "The technical term for twins by different fathers is 'heteropaternal superfecundation,' which simply means double conception, or two babies. The first case was reported by a doctor named John Archer. In 1801 Dr. Archer became the first doctor to receive a medical degree in the United States."

"Damnnnnnn!" Mae May says as she looks at the smiling babies laying back in their stroller while still shaking her head in disbelief. "This shit is crazy, damnnnn! I thought I had drama in my life but damn, my story can't touch your's!" They laugh as Mae May continues. "Cindy, I thought we were friends?" Mae May questions. Cindy is surprised by the thought and responds. "We are. How come you said that?"

"Because you never told me about Tammy's babies being Chad's and Sweets', or that Tammy had one white baby and one black one. Damn girl! I still can't believe this shit."

"I know." Cindy answers smiling. "Tammy made me promise not to tell anyone. She said it would be more fun to see the look on everyone's faces when they found out. I have to admit, your facial expression was worth a million words." They laugh.

Not Quite Good Enough

Mae May also laughs and reacts. "Ha, ha my ass! I'm sure it was." She shakes her head in disbelief again and continues. "Damn, I still can't believe this shit! But it's cool, you guys got me."

Tammy answers back, "Mae May, that's the least I could do for you is to get you back after the way you talked to me at the party."

Surprised by the response, Mae May answers, "I told you I was sorry over the phone a year ago. I thought we were cool. What's up? Are you still holding on to grudges?"

"Got ya!" Tammy laughs. "I was just saying that to get another reaction from you." they laugh.

"Damn girl, that's enough. I can't take anymore surprises today." Mae May says as they laugh.

"But don't tell the others when they get here, I want to see the look on their faces when I show them the babies!" Tammy says as Mae May and Cindy grin and agree. Tammy gives the babies a bottle and covers them back up while they go back to sleep.

Mae May still can't believe what she's seen and heard, grilling Tammy more. "Tammy, are you sure that's really what happened? You do know doctors don't know everything. Did you say you got a DNA test to prove the doctor is right?" Mae May questions and looks at Tammy with a very serious look.

Tammy laughs and responds, "Yes, I told you we did get the test because none of us could believe it either. Remember, the chances of this happening is one in a million. So I guess you could say I hit the jackpot." Tammy smiles and rocks her stroller to help the babies go back to sleep.

Mae May adds, "Well, if you ask me, I would have rather hit the lotto, instead of that kind of jackpot." They laugh as Mae May continues. "So, I guess that means our kids are not related after all?"

Tammy responds, "Well, one of them are related, just the other one isn't. But it's all good. It worked out for the best. Chad has been a wonderful father to both of the babies! He was VERY excited to see that one of the babies was his very own and he's accepted the other one just like it was his own. He loves both of them equally the same, as do I. Because of that, I love him even more. In fact, he decided to take them on the responsibility of them being his children before knowing the truth. So, if it had to be what it is, I am very pleased with the way things turned out! The only better solution to the whole thing would have been that both babies were genitally his. But since, only one is, it's cool. We love them both."

"Ahhh, that's so niceee!" Mae May says as they look at the babies together. "But that is still one of craziest stories I've ever heard in my life."

"Yeah, I know it is. But what's done is done and we're dealing with it. Chad is a great dad. We're all one big happy family." Tammy adds and continues. "He also has a great job now and takes care of us. Now I only work part time. That's only because I want to stay active in my profession."

Cindy looks at Tammy and comments with laughter. "I was just glad you let me keep my job." They laugh as she continues. "After the big blow up we had at last year's Valentine's party I knew I was history. Even though I hoped you would forgive me and give me my job back, especially knowing that I was pregnant, needed the medical benefits, and income to take care of me and baby Trina."

Tammy sneers at the comment. "Yeah, I forgave you alright by letting you be my baby's Godmommy. But don't ever pull that shit again or you'll be fired for real!" Everyone laughs.

"Where's Sophia? I thought she was coming too." Tammy asks. "I haven't seen that girl since the party last year."

"Me either." Cindy responds as she looks around the area. "She should be here soon. She called me right before I got here to say she'd be a little late. Said she was looking forward to seeing every-

Not Quite Good Enough

body again." Cindy looks up with a surprised look, "Sophia? Is that you?"

The other ladies pleasantly follow, "Sophia? Oh my God, look at you. Girl, you look good!"

"Thank you." Sophia happily twirls around in a complete circle to let the ladies observe her new look and weight loss.

"Oh my God what have you done and how can I do it, too?" Mae May asks as she gets up and twirls Sophia around to take a closer look.

"I know. How did you lose so much weight? And what size are you now?" Cindy follows.

Beaming from ear to ear, Sophia reveals how she went from a size 2X to a size 10. "Girllll, it wasn't easy but I did it! I lost 100 pounds. Now I'm a size 10, and on a real good day I can fit a size 8."

"Wow! That's great!" the ladies say in unison.

"After Brad and I got together and fell in love, I stopped eating like a pig. I used to eat just to be eating because I was lonely and depressed. Whenever I was feeling down I'd eat. After we got together, I didn't have the urge to eat like that anymore. We started working out together, which helped me tighten up all the fat rolls I had hanging. I also changed my diet by eating more healthy foods five to six times a day. I built up my metabolism and now I feel sooo much better. Brad helped me a lot with that battle. He's so wonderful to me. I love him soooo very much! I've never felt so in love in my entire life!" Sophia said, as she glows with pride.

All the ladies hug Sophia and congratulate her. "Congratulations girl. You really look good."

"Thank you. It was a lot of hard work but, with Brad's help, I felt like I could do anything."

"Girl, I'm so happy for you." Mae May adds. "I think I'll be coming to visit you soon so you can help me get rid of all my baby fat."

T' La June

"Yeah, me too." Cindy adds.

"But after having five babies it may take me awhile to look as good as you." Mae May jokes.

"Don't worry, I'll help you and when you start looking and feeling good, it'll be easier to continue."

"I feel good now, but you can still count me in for the weight lost class too." Cindy adds as Sophia nods in agreement.

"No problem, I'll help both of you. However, I won't be able to do all the exercises myself, I'll have to tell you what to do until next year, when I can fully workout with you." Sophia adds. The ladies are curious by her answer.

With a sassy tone, Mae May questions Sophia, "How come you can't workout with us? You think you're too good now that you've lost so much weight?"

Sophia smiles with a radiant glow and answers while looking down. "I'm six weeks pregnant."

"Ahhhhhhhhhhhhh!!!" the ladies say as they hug Sophia, congratulating her.

"Congratulations girl!" Mae May says. "Damn, all these surprises are making me have to pee." Everyone laughs as she continues. "Where's the bathroom?" She looks around the park. Cindy points, "It's over there."

Mae May laughs, "I'm just kidding. I don't have to pee, I was just joking, but damnnnn! Ok, no more surprises ya'll. I don't think I can handle another one without peeing on myself. But that's GREAT! Sophia, I'm happy for you and Tammy. Congratulations to both of you. You guys deserve happiness." They have another group hug.

"But I'll still be working-out while I'm pregnant. I don't want to blow up like I was before. I just won't be working out like I would have worked out if I wasn't pregnant." Sophia says as the ladies shake their heads to agree.

Not Quite Good Enough

"Surpriseeee," Vikki says as she joins the group with her girlfriend Stephanie.

"Hey girl." Everyone gives her a hug.

"We didn't know you were coming," Cindy adds.

"Sophia and I wanted to surprise you guys."

"So how are you doing?" Cindy asks as she notices Stephanie standing behind Vicki holding her hand.

"I'm good," then she looks at Stephanie, beams and says, "Everyone, this is the love of my life, Stephanie. Stephanie this is Cindy, Mae May, Tammy, and you already know Sophia."

Stephanie is beaming and extends her hand to shake. "Hello, nice meeting you all."

Mae May gives her a warm and welcoming hug, "We don't shake hands around here, we hug."

Stephanie is happy by her warmth as the others join in with hugs.

"So, what you been doing Vicki?" Mae May asks.

"Not sure if you all know, but Stephanie and I used to date a few years ago. We went our separate ways, and then at the Valentine's Day party we hooked up again. We decided that this time we wanted to be with each other, forever. We've been together ever since and we're very happy and in love. We even went to Washington, DC to get married. We had a special wedding ceremony with our close friends and family members to make it official." Vicki shows everyone Stephanie's ring as they blush.

"Ahhhhhhhhhhh, that's niceeeeeeeeee!" the ladies say in unison as the happy couple kiss and beam with pride.

"So, how are all of you doing?" Vicki asks.

"We're good." Mae May responds.

"Yes, I'm also happy." Tammy adds. "I married Chad before my babies were born and let him adopt them. I have two beautiful baby girls, Rose Marie and Marie Rose." She takes the

T' La June

blanket off the stroller and shows Vicki and Stephanie the sleeping babies. They admire them with a surprised look, but Tammy is talking so much they can't get any questions out. "We gave them our deceased grandmother's names. Chad's grandmother's name was Rose and mine was Marie. We figured if we flipped the names they would each share both of the names."

"Ahhh, they're soooo cute." Vicki says with Stephanie agreeing. "We'd like to adopt a few babies, or have one or two of them through invitro fertilization, in the near future. Right now, we're taking things slow and enjoying each other until we decide which way would be better for us. We definitely want children of our own."

"Oh my, now that's interesting." Mae May said with a surprised look on her face. "Do tell us more."

Vicki looks at Mae May ready to defend, "Yes Mae May, some gay people want kids too."

"Oh no girl, I didn't mean anything bad by what I said. I just never thought about it like that. But I guess without a man you do have to consider other options. But it's all good. If it makes you guys happy, then I'm happy." everyone smiles in agreement.

"Yeah, and when they do decide it's time to conceive, Brad and I will be the Godparents." Sophia said with pride. She winks at Vicki and Stephanie. "In fact, Brad and I are willing to donate some of Brad's sperm to help them out. But we have to find out more about the process before we do anything."

"Okkkkk, sounds good to me." Mae May hesitantly responds and continues. "I see now, this is definitely going to be a family affair."

Tammy joins in, "I think it's a great idea. Gay couples are doing the procedure more and more. I think you guys will be just fine. In fact, if you'd like, you can make an appointment with me. I can give you more information about the procedure. I will refer you all to a few great doctors who are experts in the field."

Not Quite Good Enough

"Sounds good, I'd like that." Stephanie says; her and Vicki smile. Mae May and Cindy remain quiet.

"Yes we would. I'll call you on Monday." Vicki adds as she holds Stephanie's hand and they smile with hope.

"Cindy will be in the office Monday at nine. If I'm not in yet, call and talk to her. She can give you all the information you need." Tammy suggests as she looks at Cindy who agrees.

"Yes, I'll be there. Call after 9:30 or 10 so I can get the office opened and the patients checked in. Then I'll be able to find the information you need and help you," Cindy adds.

"That will be great. We'll call after 10." Vicki and Stephanie agree.

Tammy changes the subject. "Mae May, are you still working at the shop full-time doing nails?"

"Right now I'm not working at all. I'll go back in a few months. I needed a little more time to get to know my babies, and be a mom to them. Now that I have Darren in my life, I'm trying to be something special to him as well."

"I see you cut down your nails. I never thought you'd do that." Tammy adds.

"Yeah girl, I had too once I decided I was gonna be a real mother to my kids and not a party girl. They were just too much to keep up with, without scratching the kids all the time."

"Yeah, if you ask me, they needed to be cut a long time ago." Cindy jokes and feels inside her hair as Mae May and Tammy laugh.

"So Mae May, tell us how you met Darren?" Tammy asks as everyone listens.

Mae May begins blushing, "Well, I met him one day when he delivered a package to our house. He's been our mailman for years. He knows Momma and the kids real good. Momma used to always tell me how the mailman loves my kids so much, that he comes in and plays with them for awhile before continuing his route. She said

T' La June

he also brings them treats, so they loved him already."

"Does he have kids of his own?" Tammy asks.

"Yes, he has three kids of his own, but his ex-wife has custody of them. He has visitation privileges every weekend. So we spend time together as a family when he has them."

Tammy counts on her hands all the kids and smiles as Mae May laughs and continues. "Yeah I know it's a lot of kids. With my five and his three there are eight kids between us. We have our own Brady Bunch, but it's cool. I love him and his kids. We get along as one big happy family. He treats my kids as his own since his kids are not around all the time. So now that we're a couple they love him like he's their real daddy. He's also cool with the fact that I had my tubes tied because he didn't want anymore kids either. Hell, if things do work out between us, and with all the kids we have together; we wouldn't need anymore, anyway." They laugh.

"But let me finish telling you guys how we hooked up." The ladies listen carefully as Mae May continues, "He came by my house one day to deliver a package and we started talking. He knew I had just had Re-Re so he brought her a gift. After that, we started talking and have been together ever since."

Cindy gives Mae May a fist bump. "You go girl. You didn't tell me about Darren. He sounds like a keeper."

Mae May smiles, "Yes he does and no, I didn't tell anybody about him. I wanted to see if it would work between us before I got too excited. So far it's all good. I just hope I don't jinxes things by telling you all now. It seems that I found a man who loves me for me and someone who loves all my bad ass kids." she laughs. In a serious tone Mae May says, "I've never had anyone love me the way he loves me. This has never happened to me before, and that's what makes it feel so special. It's only been a few months and everything is going great! He comes to visit the kids and we take them to the park, and

Not Quite Good Enough

Mickey D's all the time. When his kids are with us everyone gets along very well. Like I said, we're a black version of the Brady bunch. It's real cool. It's nice to have someone love you just for who you are and not try to change you, or put you down for the mistakes you made; before they came along. I never knew I could be so lucky." She starts to cry happy tears.

With tears in their eyes, Tammy and Cindy smile, hug, and utter, "Ahhhhhhhhhh, that's nice!!!"

"Well, Joe and I are still together," Cindy adds. "We're talking about getting married now. He said he can't live without me and Trina. He wants us to be a family. Sooooo, I guess I'll be getting a ring any day now. I can't wait!"

Full of excitement, together the ladies say, "You go girl."

"When we DO get married," Cindy adds. "I want all of you to be in my wedding."

"Count me in." Mae May adds.

"Me too." Sophia joins in.

"Me too, and if you guys wait awhile, our babies can also be in the wedding." Tammy suggests.

"I sure hope he doesn't take THAT damn long to propose!" They laugh as Cindy teases and continues. "The funny thing about Joe is that his mother, Mrs. Wells, is one of our patients. She told me about him being a nice guy with a crazy girlfriend over a year ago, what a small world it is. However, the best thing is that she told me he's a GREAT son and you know, great son's normally make great husbands!"

"Yes they do," the ladies agree.

"Damn, everybody's getting married." Mae May announces while feeling left out. "Sophia you married Brad. Vicki you and Stephanie are married and doing fine. Cindy, you're getting ready to marry Joe. Tammy, you and Chad are married, and we all know

183

T' La June

Marque' will always have somebody keeping him warm at night. As for me, I'm hopeful that Darren won't become disappointed in me and leave me. I love him, even though we've only been serious for a few months. My babies need a real daddy and a stable home life. I need a real man to take care of all of us. I also want someone to make me feel special everyday. I hope that happens with Darren. But hey, if it doesn't, I'll keep searching. Who knows what's in my future." Mae May looks sad. Tammy and Cindy hug her.

"It'll be alright girl." Cindy assures her.

"Yeah, I believe it'll be alright too." Tammy adds. "Darren sounds like he's the man you've been searching for a long time with your crazy ass." they laugh.

"Yeah Mae May, you're crazy as hell, but you're a good person." Cindy adds as they laugh again.

Mae May laughs and said, "I sure hope you guys are right."

"So Mae May, how's Marque'?" Tammy asks.

Mae May looks around the park, "He should be here any moment. I told him we were meeting here today. He said he wanted to see everybody to say hi."

Suddenly Marque' walks up holding hands with Jimmy. "Hey bitches! How you doin'?" Marque' said with his friendly, but crazy personality. The girls run toward him and give him a hug.

Marque' makes his introduction, "This is Jimmy, the main man in my life. I brought him by to meet the true bitches in my life," he jokes.

Jimmy extends his hand to shake, "Hello ladies."

Mae May slaps down his shake, "Hey Jimmy, good to see you again. I haven't seen you since we were in *Lotions and Motion Erotic Store* shopping for the Valentine's party. Now you know we don't do hand shakes around here, we hug those we love." Mae May hugs him and the rest of the ladies join in.

Not Quite Good Enough

"So Jimmy, you finally gave in to Marque'? I thought you had another boyfriend and was only a one man's man." Mae May says.

"I am, that's why we're together. Me and my other man broke up about a year ago. So me and Marque' have been kickin' it ever since."

"No offense to you Jimmy but I have to ask," Mae May says to Jimmy. She then turns to Marque', looking at him seriously, but with a sassy tone says, "Marque', how long will you be with Jimmy?" With her hands on her hip, she waits for an answer from Marque'. Although, before Marque' can answer, she turns to look at Jimmy and says, "Sorry Jimmy, but you know Marque', he has a new lover every few months, or every few days."

Marque' rolls his eyes at Mae May, ignores her comment, then turns Jimmy's face toward his and proceeds to tongue kiss him. The ladies look at them and smile. "Well, go on with your bad self. I ain't mad at ya'll!" Mae May responds with a big smile. "But you still didn't answer my question." She waits for an answer.

Vicki and Stephanie feel right at home after this demonstration of love in front of them, they kiss and hug each other tightly. Marque' then responds after Jimmy and him come up for air, "Not this time Mae May. This time it's serious. I proposed to Jimmy last night. We're getting married in a few months."

The ladies yell with excitement. "Yeahhh! Good for you guys." They offer hugs.

"Oh my God! I can't believe this shit. In fact, I'll believe it when I see you bitches walking down the aisle." Mae May responds.

"Jimmy, show theses bitches your ring." Marque' tells him. Jimmy holds out his hand with pride and the ladies look at his 2 carat diamond platinum engagement band.

"Marque', I'm supposed to be your best friend. You're suppose to tell me everything. Why didn't you tell me about this proposal? Hell, I've known you forever, and your ass don't go around giving 2 carat diamond rings to just anybody. So Jimmy, your ass must be special!" Mae May says while admiring Jimmy's ring with the other ladies.

Marque' smiles with a sneaky smirk. "Mae May I don't tell you every damn thing that goes on in my life. Hell, I have to keep some shit to myself every once in awhile, especially since you have such a damn big mouth." He continues as they laugh, "Now you know I've always had a thing for Jimmy, but he's been playing hard to get with me for years. Now he's mind forever."
Everyone sighs with happiness, "Ahhhh."

"Anyway, last year I invited him to the Valentines party to cheer him up. He and his man had just broken up, and he was heartbroken. Then with business slow, he got laid off from the sex store. And Mae May, since you were on maternity leave, I told Jimmy to get his manicure license. He listened to me and then took your place. Anyway, after the party, we talked about seeing if we could work out as a couple, so we started dating. Since then, we've been kicking it for almost a year. We kept our relationship to ourselves because I had to get a few more dollars out of Billy's silly ass." Marque' continues, "Anyhow, while you were on maternity leave me and Jimmy became closer. So I finally dumped Billy and decided that I wanted to spend the rest of my life with Jimmy. End of story." Marque and Jimmy kiss again.
"Ahhhhhhh, how sweettttt!!!" The ladies say in unison.

Mae May gives Marque' and Jimmy a big hug and says, "If you're happy, then I'm happy for both of you. All I have to say is thank God you finally settled your wild ass down! Lord knows, I've been telling you to settle down for awhile."

Everyone chuckles and Marque' fires back. "You can't talk bitch! Ms. Wild Ass Thang! In fact, you're the QUEEN of Ms. Wild

Not Quite Good Enough

Ass Thang!" Everyone chuckles again.

Mae May is busting up laughing and then tries to be serious. "Yeah, yeah, yeahhhh! Those were my old days. I'm through with all the partying and screwing different men all the time. I told you I was settling down with Darren. If it works out, that's what I'm going to do; settle down and I mean it. He's a real man. This time I'm making sure I do it right. I love him!"

Marque' looks at Mae May weird but serious, "Well damn, I've never heard you talk about anybody this seriously before. Hell, I'll bow down to any brotha who can settle your wild ass down. Where is he?" Marque' looks around the park in search of Darren and continues. "I must meet this brotha now to make sure he stays with you before you change your mind." Marque' bows to Mae May, while turning in a complete circle as he continues to look for Darren.

"Fuck you," Mae May teases. "Let me take a bow for your wild ass, hoe!" She laughs while bowing in front of Marque' and then toward Jimmy.

"You mean past hoe." Marque' corrects her and laughs.

Tammy and Cindy are busting out laughing. Tammy goes over to Marque'. "Ok, let's cut out all this love talk, it's getting late. Congratulations Marque' and Jimmy. I wish you both the best." She gives them another hug.

Marque' is blushing, "I wish you the same on your nuptials. Mae May told me about you and Chad getting married. I think that's great; especially after everything you've been through with Sweets. I'm glad everything worked out for you guys. I'm so happy you found a good man because Sweets wasn't good enough for any of you bitches. However, he was good enough for me!" Everyone laughs except Jimmy.

Jimmy puts Marque' in his place. "Marque' I'm here to satisfy you now. So you don't need anybody else to do a damn thang for you." Jimmy states as he grabs Marque' and passionately kisses his lips again.

"Ohhhhhhhh!" The ladies say as they laugh.

After coming up for air Marque' smiles, "Damn baby, save some for tonight." They laugh again and then Marque' gets serious with Jimmy. "I know you are baby, I'm just kidding." Jimmy barely smiles. Marque' winks at him and then looks at the ladies and says. "But for real ladies, I'm happy to see all of us happy. Hell, we all deserve happiness. And speaking of happiness, Tammy, let me see your twins."

"Here they are." Tammy says as she pulls back the blanket. The babies open their eyes when the sun hits their face.

Marque' walks over to the stroller, bends down and smiles. "Ahhh, how cute. Tammy, I thought you said you had twins. Who's babies are these? I know the black baby is yours, so who's white baby do you have and where's your other baby?"

"Those are BOTH my babies." Tammy says with a sly grin. Mae May and Cindy are trying hard to hold their laughter as Marque' attempts to figure out what they're talking about.

Marque' looks at Tammy, then at the other ladies and questions, "Ok bitches, what's really going on here? Ya'll trying to trick me or something? This shit ain't funny if that's what you're trying to do. So really, who's babies are these because I know these can't be yours and Sweets' babies. Ain't no damn way you and Sweet's can make a white baby with blond hair, blue eyes, and a black baby with black hair brown eyes. I'm not saying they're NOT cute, I'm just saying they ain't ya'll's. So, come on with the truth. I'm waiting." The lady's bump into each other howling with laughter as Marque' looks at them like they're crazy.

Sophia, Stephanie, and Jimmy go over to the babies and take a close look as well. They smile and walk away quietly while also

Not Quite Good Enough

waiting for an answer.

Marque' pulls down his sunglasses and takes a closer look. "Tammy are these YOUR babies? The one's you had with Sweet's?" Tammy, Mae May, and Cindy continue laughing as Marque' continues. "What ya'll bitches laughing at?" He looks at the ladies seriously, they look back at him saying nothing, and keep laughing.

He then takes another look at the twins, "Tammy, tell me for real, who's babies are these?"

Finally, Tammy stops laughing long enough and spills the beans about the twins and responds. "Man that was good! Mae May, Marque' got your facial expression beat by two million!" They laugh again with Marque' still looking serious. Jimmy and Sophia are wondering what's so funny about Tammy having one white, and one black baby.

Tammy stops laughing long enough to continue her explanation, "Ok, I'm sorry. I couldn't help it. But that was funny. As you can see I do have a white baby and a black baby. One baby is from Sweets. The other baby is from Chad."

Marque' is puzzled by her answer, standing with his hand on his hip waiting for the truth. "Bitch, get out of here! How can that be possible?"

Jimmy, Sophia, and Stephanie are also waiting for an honest answer. Tammy laughs while continuing with her explanation. "Ok, to make a long story short, I slept with Sweets one day, then the next day I slept with Chad. Then, I got pregnant by both of them."

"Bitch, you're lying out your ass. I ain't ever heard of no crazy shit like that." Marque' says.

Everyone is cracking up with laughter from Marque's statement. Tammy finishes her explanation. "Yes, it is crazy and yes it is true. The odds of this happening are one in a million. I just happened to hit the jackpot. Therefore, my babies have two fathers, even though they are twins."

Marque' suddenly starts laughing. "Ohhh, so I seeeee bitch! You're a hoe like the rest of us!"

Everyone laughs at his answer and Tammy confesses. "I guess you could call it something like that."

Marque' rolls his eyes and smiles. "Ummmm hummm, you fast ass thang! See, I knew your prissy ass wasn't that prefect! I knew you were a freak in the dark. I ain't mad at ya. A girls has gotta do what a girls gotta do!" He teases.
"So when did you figure out all this shit?" Marque' questions.

"When the babies were born and they came out of me looking different. So we got a DNA test to see what was actually going on." Tammy responds.

"Damnnnn, this is the craziest shit I've ever heard in my life. But hey, what the hell. As long as you love em', that's all that matters, but damnnnn that's some crazy shit!" Marque' shakes his head in disbelief as everyone laughs some more.

Tammy answers, "Marque', believe me, when they came out Chad and I were also tripping. So, it's cool. The crazy thing is that for the entire nine months of my pregnancy Chad and I believed my babies were Sweets until they were born. I never saw my ultrasound. We wanted to be surprised when they were born. So, when they came out we were surely surprised!"

"I bet you were surprised! Damnnnn, that shit is crazy!" Marque' responds. "Well, if you're happy, then I'm happy, you crazy bitch!" They roar with laughter.

Marque' questions a story he heard about Sweets. "Ok, well maybe one of you can explain a story I heard about Sweets." With puzzled looks on their faces, the ladies look at each other as Marque' continues. "I heard that one of his baby's momma's had his cute ass put in jail for failure to pay child support." He pulls down his glasses and looks at Tammy with a sly grin. "That wouldn't happen to be you

Not Quite Good Enough

Ms. Tammy would it be?"

Tammy smiles and answers, "Well, unfortunately for him I am the guilty person responsible for having his ass locked up." Everyone looks at her with surprised expressions as she continues. "That'll teach that gigolo hoe to screw me around and then laugh in my face like he did at the Valentine's Day party. Then, when I got pregnant by him again, that was just too much for me to handle and let him get away clean. He got away clean after I had Danielle, so I wasn't going to let it happen again. He forgot I'm not one of his stupid women. He also forgot that I have money to pay for a good lawyer. So, through my lawyer we were able to convince a judge to file charges for back child support for all the years Sweets never offered to take care of Danielle after knowing she was his child. Then, with the help of several of the ladies who took care of him, and those he had kids with, we were able to successfully get him convicted for being a pimp." She smiles with a sneaky smirk.

She continues, "We used several of his babies mamas who had also filed for back child support and never got paid. Of course they were more than willing to help. We were also successful in proving that he could afford to pay child support by showing his assets and bank account records." Knowing this is totally opposite from Tammy's professional demeanor, everyone is in shock with her in-dept admission.

"Now he's locked up with the same gang of hoodlums who chased him away from our hometown, because they were trying to kill his ass. Who knows if he'll even come out alive after the ten year sentence he received. So, who has the last laugh now?" Tammy beams with pride.

Everyone is quiet, while still being in shock as Marque' adds, "Preach woman! Preach!"

Mae May joins in, "Hell yeah, church is definitely in session today." She teases.

Tammy goes on, "But for real, I don't wish him too much harm while he's in there, just enough to show his ass a little payback. I had to give him what he asked for, a good screw in the ass; no pun intended, if you know what I mean." she cold-heartily says. "Call it, Sweets getting his sweet revenge." Mae May and Cindy agree and give her a fist bump gesture.

"Well, from what I've heard, he's already received some of his 'Sweet revenge.'" Marque' announces.

Tammy looks at him with a puzzled look, "How? What happened?" she asks.

Marque gladly shares his gossip, "Well, the word going around town is that Sweets has become very sweet to several of the inmates he's locked up with." Everyone looks surprised as Marque' continues while grinning. "Ummm, hummm, that's exactly what I thought when I heard the news. I heard that since he has such a great reputation of sexual healing, the inmates are taking advantage of his remarkable gift."

"Awwww." Everyone says with mixed feelings. Tammy is just smiling, keeping her thoughts and opinion to herself.

"Well Ms. Thang, is that what you were hoping for?" Marque' asks.

"I'm not surprised. It serves him right." Tammy nonchalantly answers, and continues. "Oh well, if he ever gets out of jail, he'll have to pay child support for two of my children, along with the others he has." Tammy says.

"Damn girl, you're brutal! I don't ever want to get on your bad side." Marque' says as the others shake their head in agreement. Marque' continues, "Shittt, I would have screwed him for free, with NO pain involved! Who knows, maybe when he gets out he'll be ready for me to take care of his needs. I'll hook him up the Marque' style; no pain, all pleasure, and total satisfaction. My style, he'll definitely enjoy!" Marque' points out while laughing with everyone

Not Quite Good Enough

joining in the laughter except Jimmy. Marque' looks at Jimmy and conforms him in a joking way, "Damn Baby, don't be so sensitive. You know I'm just kidding!" Marque' grabs and caresses Jimmy's behind, tickles him, and gives him a small kiss on his lips.

"Alright already. Ya'll either get a room or cut out all this damn kissing. You're making me horny." Mae May said as everyone laughs.

"What's new?" Marque' jokes. "Mae May, you're always horny," they laugh.

"Fuck you." Mae May jokingly fires back, displays her middle finger, and continues, "Well, all I'm gonna say about Sweets is that I sure will miss his joy stick. That man could screw like no man I've ever been with, that's for damn sure! Hell, he knew the how, when, where, and why, on rolling his tootsie roll all up inside a woman's coochie. Damnnnn, just thinking about how he rolls is making me horny. Ummm, I will surely miss his cute and sexy ass!" Mae May shakes her head.

"Even though I only got to enjoy it one time, I'll have to second that motion." Cindy adds and continues, "I guess he'll go down in history as my best so far."

Everyone then looks at Tammy for a confession. "What are you guys looking at me for?" She blushes. They continue looking at her while not saying a word. "Ok, okkkk! I also have to admit that, that's the ONE thing I can honesty say I'll miss about Sweets. This is why I hooked up with him again in the first place. He was my first love and no one knew how to rock my world better than him, damn." Tammy acknowledges as the other ladies agree.

"Buttttt," Vicki joins in, "Just because a man orrrrr a woman," she looks at Stephanie, smiles, and continues, "can rock your world, doesn't mean we should excuse them and/or give him or her our entire world. That's one of the main reasons women pass up good men or women. They're constantly comparing them to the ONE who could rock their world the best." Everyone kind of agrees as she continues. "Come on people, think about it like this, if he or she was doing what was right the first time around, or had the entire package to make us completely happy, we never would have let them go in the first place." Everyone looks around and fully agrees. "Soooo, my suggestion is for everyone to find a man, or a woman, who makes them happy for the long haul, instead of settling for someone who can only satisfy our temporary needs." Everyone looks at her strangely, "Wait a minute, I'm not trying to be goodie-two-shoes. I truly understand that sometimes we have to do what we have to do in order to get what we want. But, don't do it at the expense of hurting or losing a good man or woman." Everyone smiles in agreement.

"Damn, preach sista, preach!" Mae May teases. "I need to start going to both of ya'll's church. What time are services on Sunday?" She laughs.

Vicki laughs back and shakes her head as Mae May looks at Tammy and changes the subject. "Tammy, whatever happened with the kid you had when you were in high school?"

"Danielle's seventeen now and in college. She's a smart and sweet young lady. She advanced in her grades when she was young and she's an honor student. I love her dearly. I always stayed in touch with her and took care of her. My mother just took care of her while I earned my degree. Once I moved here to California, to pursue my own practice, she didn't want to leave her friends, so she stayed with my mom. It was her choice, not mine, to stay with my mom. I just made the decision to not talk about her. I didn't want people to judge me for having a baby while I was in high school. I figured I could get more respect if they didn't know I made a mistake. But it's all good. No real damage was done, except that she was unable to know her no good daddy. I never thought he was good enough for her anyway. I didn't want to push the issue of him meeting her while she was grow-

Not Quite Good Enough

ing up. When she got old enough to understand, my mom and I always told her about him. She's the one who chose not to meet him. Now, if she wants to meet him she can go to his jail cell, without me. She's old enough to make reasonable decisions. She doesn't need me to hold her hand. She can do whatever she pleases with or without my help. If she decides to meet him and she needs me to be there with her, I'm there!" Everyone shakes their head in agreement with Tammy. The babies start crying.

Marque' looks at them and plugs up his ears. "Well THAT'S my cue to get the hell on out of here. Babies are something that definitely won't be in my master plan! See you bitches later!" He kisses each of them on their cheek and gives them a hug goodbye. Jimmy does the same thing.

"Dammit Marque', my babies are in your plan. Remember, you're their Goddaddy," Mae May reminds Marque'.

"Yeah they are and I love them to death. But I can take their little bad ass's home when I've had enough." He smiles and puts his hands in the air, gesturing enough. "See ya later bitches!" Everyone gives each other hugs, and waves goodbye. Marque' and Jimmy walk away happy and in love, with their hand inside each other's back pocket.

Tammy is holding one of her babies, rocking her so she won't cry. "Well that's my cue to leave as well. Chad will be home from work soon and I want to have dinner ready when he gets there." She lays the baby down with a bottle and prepares to leave.

"Yeah, we're gonna get out of here too ya'll" Vicki adds and gives everyone a hug. "It was good seeing all of you again. We'll have to get together soon. Tammy, I'll call your office on Monday."

"Ok, Cindy will make the appointment and set you up with a great doctor."

"Thanks, we really appreciate that."

"Yes we do." Stephanie adds. "It was nice meeting all of

you. I look forward to seeing you soon."

"Same here, nice to meet you." the girls respond back.

"Good luck to you guys. I'll wait for your call," Cindy adds. "Ok ya'll, I'm out of here, too. Joe is over my house more than he's at his own house. So I better get dinner together before he comes home. I'll talk to you gals later." She packs up her baby to leave.

"Ladies, it's been nice." Mae May said as she calms down her baby with a bottle. "Let's meet more often. This was fun."

"Yes it was." Cindy admits. "Love you bitches!" They smile as everyone exchanges hugs and goes their separate ways.

The end!!

FRONT COVER MODEL

Dorian Drake Jr./Owner of Fade II Black Ent.
Model/ Exotic Entertainer

Dorian has appeared in several Movies, Television Commercials, Calendars and Music videos.

Fade II Black provides entertainment for ladies such as Male Revue Club Shows, Birthday, Bachelorette, Divorce or just because parties.
Also available for modeling and print work.

To inquire about bookings:
Dorian Drake
(619) 788-3233

drakedorian04@gmail.com
www.myspace.com/fade2blackent.
www.facebook.com/doriandrakejr

PUBLICATION ORDER FORM

MAIL ORDERS TO: TM Publications, Orders Dept.
PO Box 2099, Sun City, CA 92586

Please Print:

Name:_____

Address:_____

City:_____ State_____ Zip_____

Telephone:(   )_____ fax (   )_____

Email Address:_____

PRICES ARE PER BOOK:

$3.00 S&H for 1st book/ $1.50 S&H for each additional book shipped together within the US ONLY.

Sales Tax: Add 8.50% for products shipped to California.

Not Quite Good Enough / Novel $14.99 x_____ $_____
978-0-9713221-5-8

Unbreakable, A Guide to Understanding Marriage and Relationships / Novel   978-0-9713221-2-7 $14.99 x_____ $_____

Mind Games /   Novel 0-9713221-1-2 $14.95 x_____ $_____

Mind Games / CD $19.99 x_____ $_____

How To Self Publish on a Shoestring Budget! $9.99 x_____ $_____

-In 10 Easy Steps - Instructional Booklet 0-9713221-9-8

Momma, Please Forgive Me! / Novel $13.95 x_____ $_____
0-9713221-0-4

Shipping Total $_____

Sales Tax Total $_____

Grand Total $_____

Visit website for Credit Card Orders: www.toimoore.com

For Multi-Book discounts or Fund Raisers,
contact tmpublications1@aol.com

Other Books by author

TOI MOORE

UNBREAKABLE, A GUIDE to UNDERSTANDING MARRIAGE and RELATIONSHIPS

ISBN: 978-0-9713221-2-7   Retail Price $14.99   Released Winter 2005
A book describing how *Greg* and *Toi* have been married for over 20 years and are still in love. It reveals their personal and private life while doing the best they could do to make their life complete. It's raw, sassy, and on the edge. There are no prim or proper techniques, nor is there any finger pointing or blaming one mate over the other, or insisting that one gender is better than the other. A must have book for any couple trying to find answers as to what they can do to make their relationship work.

MOMMA, PLEASE FORGIVE ME!

ISBN: 0-9713221-0-4   Retail Price $13.95   Released Fall 2001
A story that depicts how an African-American woman was in an abusive relationship with her husband. This dynamic story details how a woman committed murder in order to protect herself and her children. It describes how her actions caused more pain than solutions. It also sheds a light on how domestic violence is considered a silent killer and why it should be stopped! After reading my book, it will shed more details and understanding as to why La Vonne did what she did in order to save herself and her children.

MIND GAMES

ISBN: 0-9713221-1-2   Retail Price $14.95   Released Fall 2003
The sequel to *Momma, Please Forgive Me!* explores the after effects of how a woman, who has been separated from her family for over ten years, comes back into society and tries to live a normal and happy life. However, there are many twists and turns in this story as she tries to be the perfect mother to her now teenage children. This story explores the daily lives of how La Vonne's children treat her and how their classmates treat them after finding out the hidden truth of what their mother did and why she has been out of their lives for so long.

HOW TO SELF PUBLISH ON A SHOESTRING BUDGET IN 10 EASY STEPS

ISBN: 0-9713221-9-8   Retail Price $9.95   Released Spring 2001
An instructional booklet that shows how readers can publish their own book without spending a lot of money. Everyone has that great story of knowledge to share with others that can make them a million dollars. However, many don't know how to make their writings into a published book on their own. Now, they can create that book and seek that million dollar pay check that has their name on it *In 10 Easy Steps*. These facts have been proven true, because the author has used them herself.

BOOK ARTIST

Leonard D. Ragsdale
ragsdale.leonard@yahoo.com

Born: Leonard D. Ragsdale on August 11, 1978 in St, Louis, MO. Raised in Los Angeles, California, now living in "The Crossroads of the U.S.A." Wentzville, MO.

Inspiration:
God giving me this day to be better than it was the day before.

"I've been drawing all my life as a way to release my inner feelings. It wasn't until my mother, Sharon D. Ragsdale, took some of my sketches and showed me how to make and sell T-shirts that I began to draw things for people. It was those T-shirts that kept money in my pocket. It also kept me too busy to get into trouble, while allowing precious time to spend with my mom.

From pencil to spray-can, I've had my hand on it. I never tried to imitate or humiliate anyone. Besides GOD, I want my wife and kids to be my biggest fan. Thank you so much Toi!" Len

**"I cry so hard I laugh,
I laugh so hard, I cry!"**

Len 2006

BACK COVER MODEL

JOHN BRICE

For more information or a resume'

contact:

john.globalmediapartners@gmail.com

LOOKING FOR A SPEAKER?

Toi Moore is that special speaker who will enhance your lecture series and/or other observances!

"Leave it up to Toi L. Moore to keep it real on love, relationships, and accomplishments. She's a dynamic and delightful writer, as well as a hell of a woman!" *Vivica A. Fox* / **Actress**

Toi Moore, is the author of: **Not Quite Good Enough; Mind Games; Unbreakable, A Guide to Understanding Marriage and Relationships; Momma, Please Forgive Me!;** and **How to Self Publish on a Shoestring Budget -10 Easy Steps Mind Games.** She is a frequent writer for *Billboard, Upscale and Turning Point* Magazines to name a few. As a speaker, she offers uplifting and powerful messages about: Domestic violence, Relationships, Writing, Interviewing, Self publishing and Motivational topics.

The topics spoken by *Toi Moore* are filled with personal tragedies and tramps that will enlighten, encourage and educate her audiences. Allow Toi Moore to articulate the concerns of many people around the world. *Toi Moore* is available for lectures, conferences and workshops. Feel free to contact her by visiting her website at: **www.toimoore.com,** email: tmpublications1@aol.com, or through mail at: TM Publications, PO Box 2099, Sun City, CA. 92586-2099. 951-231-1633 We look forward in hearing from you soon!

Toi Moore is also available for book club events and appearances.

Check out Toi Moore on Facebook at: Toi Moore's Fan Page www.toimoore.com